SONG ON A LOOP

Song On A Loop

Spiderwize
Remus House
Coltsfoot Drive
Woodston
Peterborough
PE2 9BF

www.spiderwize.com

A CIP catalogue record for this book is available from the British Library.

The views expressed in this work are solely those of the author and do not necessarily reflect the views of the publisher, and the publisher hereby disclaims any responsibility for them.

All characters in this publication are fictitious and any resemblances to real people either living or dead are purely coincidental.

ISBN: 978-1-911596-80-6

SONG ON A LOOP

LILY KRAMER

SPIDERWIZE
Peterborough UK
2018

Turning over old memories is like turning over old crusted earth. The territory you reveal is rich, fertile and moist but vulnerable with new exposure.

Turning over old memories is like tearing open old wounds, old hurts, discovering old roots which infiltrate past lands. The deeper the spidery threads burrow, the harder they are to pull up and treat.

Turning over old memories reminds you of who you really are.

CONTENTS

Alison 1

Dorothy 14

The Meeting 17

Marriage, Birth and Decline 47

The Accident 76

The Birth 83

Snippets of the childhood of Alison Benson 90

James 117

Marriage, Birth and Decline 120

Breaking the Shackles 137

Snippets of a New Life 151

Harry 157

The Reunion 161

The Meeting 187

Marriage, Redemption and Hope 197

Reflection 202

Peace 206

CHAPTER 1

Alison
2012

Desperate for a breather I step out of the meeting and, Jesus, it gets me every time. The ground, seven floors below, visible through the thick glass platform, swims up to greet me. I steady myself and take my eyes away from the floor, away from the swirling confusion of vertigo. I edge my way to the corridor where I can find refuge in coffee and solitude. The walls close in around me and I see my distorted image in the brass of the handrail. It dances while my head becomes bigger, then smaller, morphing into Eduard Mulch, 'The Scream'. This place has the power to knock me sideways at any given moment, to steal my breath like a thief. Chrome, glass, and black-marbled wonder; the overt representation of a life well spent, of decisions well-made and of drive, confidence and self-assured conviction. I'm a world away from where I was.

A sharp dig in the shoulder stirs me from my reverie and I turn to see Dominic Matthews, heir to this empire, his privilege oozing from every pore. My eyes hold his for a second too long and I mentally kick myself.

"Hey gorgeous, can't take the pace?" he asks. Conceited git.

"I'm just a woman Dom," I say, flashing my best, enigmatic 'is it a smile or a smirk?' look. I straighten up and turn sharply, my stiletto grinding into marble. I can almost feel the resentment following me like poison in the wind, ready to floor me, should I allow it. Dominic Matthews is not used to anything but fawning adoration from the women who surround him and he hates to be ignored.

As I step back into the conference room I realise, with relief, that most people have gone and the meeting is all but over. I collect my note pad and smile at doodles scribbled earlier, during particularly tedious and rambling speeches. I collect the Perspex holder that reminds me and tells everyone else, who I am; Alison Benson, Senior Partner. The cold glance which Amy Dwyer casts my way doesn't go unnoticed but I pretend not to see and I make my way back to the office.

The opulence of the place still knocks me off kilter and it takes a big effort to divert my thoughts from their journey to the past. I use the technique I have honed over the years to clear my mind of detritus; deep breaths in, longer breaths out. A rap at the door snaps me back to the present and I beckon for whoever it is to come in, then wish I hadn't. Amy Dwyer stands before me, her blonde locks, straightened to perfection, framing the glowing beauty of her face. If she smiled, she'd be lethal, as it stands, she's just stunning.

"Hi Amy, what can I do for you?" I ask, my professionalism masking my inner response.

"Oh, it's just that me and Dom are having drinks after work tonight and wondered if you'd like to join us?"

'Me and Dom,' I mimic in my head. Silly bitch thinks

she's really caught the slippery toad but I, for one, know better.

"What's the celebration?" I ask, knowing her agenda, she just wants to gloat and show him off; he who is Mr. Desirable, the most sought-after shag in the firm.

"Nothing much, just seems like ages since we got together, that's all," she replies, pushing her hair back from her forehead and looking down at me through the flickering fan of false lashes.

"Well look, I've got so many documents to browse, it's not even funny, but if I get through a decent amount, I might see you there. Cross Keys?"

"Yeah," she says, "about seven."

She pushes out her ample chest, sucks in her tiny midriff and lazily ambles out, her pert little arse swaying as she goes. She stops for a moment, flicks her head sharply back to face me and throws me the very merest hint of a smile. It's her eyes though, that say it all; 'keep away from him, you can never compete with me.' 'Poor cow,' I think; she really believes she's everything he wants. She doesn't suspect that, soon enough, he'll cast her aside like he has done all the others, bored with the banal exchanges and self-adoration.

I wasn't lying about the amount of work to get through and I pick up the first folder, a new case; some woman trying to sue the NHS for negligence. Dominic dropped it by earlier with a brief verbal outline of the history. The woman in question is dying of bowel cancer, metastases just about everywhere and three kids to feed. It seems she had symptoms for years but the GP put it down to Irritable Bowel Syndrome and didn't investigate until it was too late. I can't help but think about the futility of taking this case on; there's little chance of it being settled before this poor woman dies, if it can ever be settled at all. The best we can hope for is that her kids will be well cared for, financially at least.

As I pull back the manila cover, a name swims up and knocks the stuffing out of me. I lose control of my heartbeat and a band of pressure threatens to crush my chest. I stand and pace the room, not knowing what to do, until I'm forced to sit down by the dizziness of panic. An elephant sits on my chest rendering me immobile for a moment. I look at the name again and slowly roll it around my tongue, but it doesn't change into someone else's. I frantically skim the page for clues. The date of birth confirms my worst fears and I'm blindsided by images that I haven't asked for and don't want; I'm powerless to move. The past I've buried so well, for so long, threatens to rise from its murky depths and strangle me.

The palpitations make me giddy and I walk over to get water from the dispenser, trying in vain to gather my thoughts as I go. Gone is my confident stride, replaced by a slow shuffle and the hunched shoulders of my youth. Inside I'm flapping around like an escaped balloon. I need to reign it in, to regain my form. I take a sip of cool water but it makes me retch, so I ease myself back into my seat and sit stock-still for I don't know how long.

I thought I'd made the perfect escape, thought they'd never find me here, in Brighton. I wanted to be as many miles away from my beginnings as I possibly could. How cruel fate is that it should send a sibling so far south, to seek out the changeling sister, and in such dire

4

circumstances. I think of something one of my therapists once said; 'You can run but you can't hide'. How bloody true.

Dominic's uninvited entry makes me look up and he flinches at the sight of me.

"Hey Alison, what's wrong babe? You look like you've just caught a glance of old man Matthews himself, come to haunt us."

'No,' I think, 'the ghosts I am about to meet are much more sinister than that.'

Before I can protest, Dominic moves behind and starts to massage my shoulders in a spontaneous show of support and affection. It makes me want to scream, 'leave me the fuck alone,' but instead I crumple and the tears flow.

"Hey, you really are upset, aren't you?" he asks, with genuine concern and it strikes me that an ex-conquest, someone I thought meant nothing to me and vice-versa, cares more than I like to acknowledge. I slump further down into the chair trying to become invisible again, to go back to where I was a couple of hours ago, when my life was on track.

Dominic's back rub lasts about two minutes before I politely tell him to sod off. Who needs a social viper when your world's about to be ripped apart? I don't know how long I've been here like this but the office now seems eerily quiet. I've not seen or heard a soul since Dominic went, which probably means I'm the only one left. I need to move, if only to stretch my legs and restore my exterior, at least, to some sort of normality. I step into the adjacent wash room, look in the mirror and thank God I didn't have to pass any of the others with a face like this. Black streaks lace their way down puffy cheeks; how Amy Dwyer would gloat if she saw me now. I think about her as I clean away the remnants of make-up, think about how false she is with her implants, hair extensions, ridiculous brows and rubber doll lips. Am I any better? If I fused her fake body with my fake life, would I even exist at all?

As I reapply make up I think about damage limitation, a term I'm familiar with in this profession; how I can stop this from destroying everything I have come to know? How can I avoid a future meeting with my past and everything it will bring? I'm used to finding answers, sorting out dilemmas, but this one is beating me.

When I calm down enough to function, I finish applying my mask and feel slightly better. Any papers needing attention will have to wait until tomorrow, I can't face anything that requires any amount of thought or effort. I look at the girl in the mirror and a frightened child looks back. I need to take back control. I need a drink. Mature response or not, I've got to escape from this negative mindset before it drags me under. A glass of wine will lift my mood enough to make a start.

I gather my things, the image on the plastic ID card mocks me; 'Take a last look,' it says, 'you're about to disappear.' The thought of losing who I am makes the need for a drink more urgent. I stride out to the main office and pass row upon row of empty desks. It must be after nine, at least, even the die-hard workaholics have gone. The lift takes me smoothly down to reception and Tom looks up and nods his head in recognition.

"Night Tom," I say as evenly as I can, "see you tomorrow."

"Good Night Alison," he responds, as he opens the main glass door.

I step out into the grey of the late-evening and tread the familiar route to salvation. The rush hour has passed and there isn't the usual throng of people going for the bus or train that I usually see when I leave at a more respectable hour. I'm so distracted that I nearly trip over the homeless person and join him on his tatty blanket. Perhaps it's the fear of losing my identity that makes me reach for the change in my purse. I crouch down to drop it gently into his bucket.

"Thanks love," he says.

I look at the bearded man, almost disappearing inside the furry hood of his grubby parka and, for once, I wonder what his story is. I'm tempted to crawl under the blanket with him, share tales and get absolutely smashed. Instead I hold his hand and pat his shoulder, then I walk towards the bright light of the neon sign which beckons me to come forward, towards oblivion.

The place is buzzing with chat and laughter and I'm relieved to reach the counter without being recognised or harassed. On any other day, I would stand confidently, shouting my order above the clamour of evening drinkers, but tonight I slip quietly to the edge of the revellers, self-consciously waiting for the bartender to notice me. For what seems like an age I stand there imagining that I am transparent, that people can see right through to my core, to my grubby secrets. Finally, I catch his eye and order a large drink and, when it arrives, the honey liquid drops easily down my throat and I wish I'd ordered two. I savour the taste and take a second gulp, closely followed by a third. I wait for a second or two for the drink to take effect, but it doesn't, so I raise my hand and order another.

"Looks like you needed that," I hear someone say.

One of the 'suited and booted' brigade is slouched on the stool next to me. Typical of the men who come in here, he looks like he's worked hard and drank harder.

"You could say that," I say, and, not wanting to talk, I turn my back on him.

I can feel his miserable eyes boring a hole into my back. Most of the men in here have egos to match their cars; big and invincible. No need to chase a stroppy fifty-something when there are plenty of young things around.

I could down that second glass in one, but I resist. As much as I want to 'drink to forget' I choose instead to sip and savour. As the effect of the wine weaves its magic, I feel an incongruous smirk rise at each corner of my mouth at the thought of what is about to unfold. I make my way to the back of the room and find a seat in the corner. I hold my wine like it's treasure, not wanting to put it down for fear it might disappear. I run my finger down the side of the glass and move my face closer, then further, closer, then further, but 'The Scream' isn't there this time, just a fuzzy image. Someone is looking at me curiously and I realise I must look deranged, so I put the wine down gently. He takes the seat next to me.

"Sorry to disturb your little love affair with your crisp white, but I thought you might like some human contact?"

"Whatever gave you that impression? I may look like a bit of a sad case, but I'm not about to be whisked away in a van just yet."

"Sorry, I didn't mean to imply that you're mad or anything, it's just that I saw you come in and you looked quite devastated about something. Then when your first drink didn't touch the sides, I thought you might have had some bad news, thought you might want to talk. I'm sorry, I don't mean to pry. I'm Jack, by the way."

I look him in the eye, trying to fathom whether he's worthy of my time, whether I should tell him where to go or allow him into my confidence. I think he may be right about wanting to talk and who better to talk to than a stranger? Besides, I don't have to tell him everything.

"Bad news is a bit of an understatement I'm afraid, but my crisp white friend is helping a bit. She's more fruity than crisp, actually. With honey undertones."

"Really? What's her name?"

"Chardonnay."

"Good choice. Want another?"

"Why the hell not?"

While he's at the bar I finish the rest of the drink. I'd normally stop at two large glasses, especially on a week night. Tonight's more like a 'weak night', I think, and I've no intention of stopping just yet. The glow is rising now and I can feel its fuzzy blanket warming me.

"You're smiling, that's progress," he says as he returns with the drink and places it next to my empty glass.

I resist reaching for it straight away, don't want him to think I'm some sort of lush who makes a regular habit of this. Not that it's any of his business and not that I care.

"Thanks for that. I love a good Chardonnay. I see you've gone for red."

"I prefer a red, especially a Merlot. I like the fruity, oaky tones. I like the warmth of it as it slips down your throat. Oh, that sounded a bit rude, didn't it? What have we here then? One old lush and a rusty old letch."

"Less of the old if you don't mind," I say and, to my surprise, I find myself giggling at his comment.

Three glasses become four, then five and when I get up, I feel so unsteady that I need to sit down again for a few seconds. Using the tables to regain balance, I make my way slowly across the bar and push open the first door. The stench hits me first, then the sight of pinstripe trousers nudges my awareness and I stop. I hear a stifled laugh and realise I'm in the Gent's. I stumble out and through the next door, entering inelegantly. A row of beauties crane their necks to see what the fuss is about, then continue with their preening, the sight of a sad, middle-aged woman tottering in, being nothing of note. I use the toilet and wash my hands, managing to splatter myself spectacularly in cold water. I stand under the hand-dryer, wafting my blouse and rubbing at the wet patch on my skirt, trying to regain my dignity, so that I don't go out looking like I've wet myself. The thought makes me giggle but when I catch sight of myself in the mirror, I am almost rendered sober. Hair dishevelled, mascara smudged and clothing askew, I wouldn't look out of place under that blanket after all.

There is one girl remaining from the row of 'preeners' and, seeing the look of shock on my face, she offers me a hairbrush and a smile which says 'we've all been there'. I brush my locks back to something which resembles 'acceptable'; if only I could do that with my life. With a damp tissue, I remove the black smudges from around my eyes, then apply a fresh coat of lipstick. My beautiful silk blouse is marred by unsightly water stains, so I tuck it into my skirt and reach underneath to pull it down. Despite my best efforts, the blouse, stuffed into an already tight skirt, ruins the smooth line, so I yank it out again. Now it's both crumpled and sullied.

My mood has changed from buoyant to morose and I slump back to my seat, edging too close to my new 'companion'. He shuffles discretely away muttering something about space invaders and giggling into his drink. Suddenly he's not sophisticated, but stupid and I wonder what I'm doing here.

"Maybe I should go," I say and I pat the side of my seat in search of my handbag.

"Maybe you should stay," he says, "just for one more. It's been fun, let's have one for the road."

"One for the road, but then I really need to go," I concede.

He goes to the bar and I'm left, staring into my empty glass as if I can will it to be full again. Someone approaches, a girl with tanned, spindly legs and I look up to see Amy Dwyer, hand on hip looking down at me from her gilded, princess tower. Her screeching voice hurts my ears.

"We missed you at the Cross Keys."

"Fuck off," I say and she shuffles off, but not before I see the shock register on her perfect face; even Botox couldn't stop that one. I stick my middle finger up at her as she shimmies off to join Dominic and his cronies, no doubt. My friend returns with the drink, my finger isn't retracted quickly enough.

"Steady! What's that for? I've only bought you a drink."

"It wasn't aimed at you. It was aimed at her."

"At who?"

"At Amy fucking Dwyer," I say.

"Name rings a bell," he says.

"She probably has."

"What?"

"Rang your bell," I say, "and the rest."

We collapse into a fit of giggles, which somehow results in an embrace. As I shake with laughter in the arms of this stranger, I catch sight of Dominic striding past and looking at us in disbelief and disgust, Amy Dwyer hanging off his arm like a spider monkey.

Our laughter subsides and we sit there for a minute, sipping our drinks and staring ahead.

I awake to the sound of a tea cup rattling in its saucer and I open one eye, fearful of where I might be. Thankfully, or not, I'm at home, I just don't remember getting there. My husband, Harry, is looming over me.

"You not going in work today then?" he asks.

"Why, what time is it?"

"About three hours later than when you rolled in," he replies, standing over the bed like a bad omen.

"It was a tough day, I went for a drink, it's not a crime," I say, not wanting to dwell on it.

"It must have been tough judging by how many drinks you had. You were so bladdered, you couldn't even find your key, never mind put it in the door."

"Yeah well, sounds familiar," I reply, wondering if he'll get the innuendo.

He does and his face drops. He slumps away, back to his office and I sit up, grateful to be alone.

"Thanks for the tea," I say and stifle a giggle, even though my head feels like it's splitting in two.

'I must still be drunk,' I think and then I remember Merlot Man. I close my eyes, and groan, remembering one or two 'flashbacks'. I vaguely remember leaving the bar, struggling down the steps, him holding me up, but have no idea what happened next. No doubt I made an idiot of myself, but that's the least of my worries. The clock says ten past eight. I'm normally engrossed in paperwork by now, on my third coffee. I swing my legs out of bed and a well of acid rises. I just about make it to the loo, where I spew the entire contents of my stomach into the bowl. Maybe I'll feel better now. I clean up the bathroom and myself, not liking the grey person who looks back at me from the mirror. I wonder if my face will crumble as it takes on all the wrongs from my former life, like The Portrait of Dorian Gray. I wonder what will happen when my past catches up with me.

Chapter 2

Dorothy

2017

Dorothy wonders how, at the age of eighty-seven, she's ended up on her own with only her things. The keyboard mocks her from the corner of the room, a sad replacement for a life never fully lived. She had to turn to music as an escape from the crippling emptiness. She has no home, just three rooms that she occupies in this 'complex'. She laughed when they called it that, it sums up her life.

She has everything she needs, but nothing she wants. The 'shrine' to two of her boys who were taken too young gives her no comfort. The photographs only serve to remind her of what was and what could have been. Her girls beam down at her from the picture on the wall, given to her by the youngest. Their smiles hide the lives they've had. Bad beginnings, just like her and not always the happy endings they hoped for. There's one missing from the picture, Alison. Dorothy wonders what became of her. 'Funny kid that,' she thinks.

Her children don't know the half of it, what she's been through. They don't know about the hardship of her early life in that bug-infested terrace, with that mare of a woman who called herself a mother. They don't know that her life was mainly a journey of abuse and sadness. She's bounced back from it all, but they don't know. They don't come to see her very much, if at all. The eldest lad rings when he wants something, normally money. The others don't bother. She'd like them to come, especially now she's in here. Everyone else seems to have visitors every week; children, grand-children, friends. Ironic really, Dorothy thinks. Of all the people in here, she probably has the most kids and grand-kids of them all, but they don't come. They used to come, full of questions. Why this and why that. They never seemed to be happy with the answers.

Age is creeping up on me, thinks Dorothy. Age, illness and loneliness. Everything aches, everything hurts, but nothing aches and hurts more than this old, lonely heart. This heart that was always looking to be fixed by a happy ending.

I never got my happy ending, she thinks. In fact, she reflects, I've never been happy. From the day I was born, to this minute right now, I can't remember ever being happy.

Dorothy thinks about the times she cared for her sister. The times they'd go out in the depths of Winter, with only a flimsy frock and a moth-eaten cardigan, no socks and clogs which were too big. They'd look for anything they could scavenge to keep the hunger at bay, but there wasn't much around. Her sister would cry with the cold and Dorothy would rub her hands to get them warm, but it never worked. She'd always have a snotty nose and her feet would slide around in her clogs which were handed down. Now and again, early in the morning, they'd see a family pushing a loaded cart down the street, always with a bucket swinging from the handle. Her mother said they were 'doing a moonlight' because they couldn't pay the rent. Hard times. At night time, in bed, they'd have to wrap a scarf around their heads to stop the bugs crawling down their ears. It would be freezing and they'd shiver under the blankets, trying to get warm. It's no wonder she had bronchitis three times and was sent away to recover. She remembers the house in North Wales with great fondness. She didn't want to leave. The other kids would be snivelling about missing home and missing their parents, but Dorothy was happy in her own bed with new clothes to wear.

Dorothy's mother was a bit of a 'card'. While her husband was away in Burma, doing what he could for his country, she would bring men home, thinking she'd get away with it, but Dorothy was not stupid. She saw everything. She confronted one of them once and told him he's better watch out or else her dad would punch him when he got back.

Dorothy wrote to her father, telling him all about school, but not about the men. His letters back always included a poem he'd written just for her. That was the light that kept her going. He was a lovely, caring man. When he returned from Burma, he asked Dorothy whether any other men had been in his house. She looked him in the eye and said, 'no dad.'

Life got better for Dorothy when she started work. There were the dances at Belle Vue and the dalliances with young men. Glimmers of happiness. Then she met *him* ....

Chapter 3

The Meeting
1948

A thief stole her breath every time she saw her own reflection. Such a stunner looked back from the looking glass, 'look but don't see.' In her mind, Dorothy was as plain as any girl could ever be, with nothing much of any interest to say either. The girl in the mirror was self-assured and beautiful, with eyes that saw everything, eyes that cut through to the soul with grave accuracy. The girl in her soul was dull and saw nothing, knew nothing. If only the image in her mind's eye would marry with the one in the mirror, then she could have a 'happy ever after' instead of a 'who'd want me?'

She snapped out of her reverie, reached for her lip liner and glided it skilfully around the outline of her mouth forming a Cupid's Bow at the top. She filled in the outline with the bold new lipstick she had bought yesterday; pillar box red, not her usual pink. She pouted at her reflection and hoped she didn't look like too much of a floozy with the red lips, not least to keep her mother from throwing that word and others at her as she went out. She could do without it, felt bad enough as it was, doubted herself enough without her mother's input.

A knock at the door made her start. That must be

Joan calling for her, ready for their Friday night out. She afforded herself one last glance through the mirror, one last assessment of her outer shell, the inner self buried like a hermit crab. Even through her self-critical eyes, she could see that she looked good. Her pencil skirt clung tightly to her slim thighs and showed off the curve of her bottom perfectly. The jacket she had chosen flattered her figure; showed off the roundness of her bosom, the breadth of her shoulders and her narrow waist. She twisted round once more to check the seams of her stockings, then she grabbed her handbag and went downstairs. She didn't want to risk facing her mother and the disapproving looks, so she headed straight for the front door.

"Tarra Mam, Dad," she shouted down the lobby where she waited for the backlash. She heard no response, so she slipped quietly out of the house, closing the door gently and turning around to greet her friend.

"God Joan, you don't know how much I'm gasping for a drink. I've had the day from hell and me mam's proper getting on me nerves. She never has a nice word to say and the house stinks like shite. Take me away from all this and let's have some fun. Me poor father to be stuck in there with that mare of a woman. God help him."

"Come on, it can't be that bad," said Joan, "Either way, it doesn't matter now. We're free, if only for a night and I'm going to have the biggest port and lemon you've ever clapped your eyes on, 'cos I've earned it this week."

"Make that two, extra-large ones at that. I can't wait to get on that floor and dance this week away. Who knows, I might even meet a handsome stranger and get whisked away to Wonderland".

"Are you kidding?" asked Joan, "The nearest we'll get to Wonderland is soddin' Woolworths!"

They laughed and trotted along the street towards the bus stop, linking arms and swapping tales, giggling like school girls trading secrets. The toils and frustrations of the week slowly dissipated and they looked forward to an evening of music, dancing and, above all, freedom.

They arrived at Belle Vue Dance Hall, joined the queue and chatted while they waited to get in. Too vain to wear thick winter coats, they shivered as the November chill hung around them and stung their work-worn hands. Their short jackets may have accentuated their trim waists, but they were no contest for the biting winter wind which whipped around them, making them wish that the people in front would hurry up. They clung to each other for warmth and support, comparing their outfits, their working weeks and vowing to wear their 'big' coats next time.

After a long, cold wait, they finally got in and made their way through to the main bar and dance floor, holding on to each other for reassurance. It was dim but they could see that some people were up already, gliding, gyrating and twirling to the music while the band belted out Glen Miller's In the Mood. Some girls, braver than Dorothy, were dancing alone, others danced with partners; they all looked happy. Dorothy wondered when she would find this happiness that everyone else seemed to have. She couldn't wait to get up there herself and join the others in their happy dances, but she'd need a drink first to quell the nerves. As they approached the bar, they heard a commotion at the entrance and they looked to see what the fuss was about. A group of men had arrived by coach, spilling noisily onto the car park. Dorothy squinted, as if this would help her to get a better look. She stopped and gripped Joan's arm as one of them caught her eye. He was tall and stocky, smartly dressed and had a distinct cleft down the centre of his chin. His hair was dark with a quiff, Brylcreemed to perfection and 'Oh Lord,' thought Dorothy, 'a smile that would stop clocks and hearts.'

There was no doubt he was handsome but, despite being in the company of a few others, he looked a bit self-conscious the way he kept casting his gaze down to the ground. 'Hey up lad, there's nowt to see down there,' she felt like saying; 'look at me!' Then he gave her a half-smile as he caught her staring at him and her stomach flipped like her mother's dolly tub on wash day. Joan wrenched her back to reality and towards the bar. They ordered drinks and, as soon as they were placed on the brass counter, Dorothy took a long sip and smiled as the warmth of it hit her senses.

"That's better," she said.

"I thought you were going to pass out then, for a minute. Who were you looking at?" asked Joan.

"What do you mean, who was I looking at? Did you not see him, the one with the Robert Mitchum chin?"

"No, I didn't, all I saw was a bunch of fools falling off a coach."

"They may be fools Joan, but they're handsome fools. Don't make it obvious, but he's on the other side of the bar."

"That's where he can stay an' all, for all I care," said

Joan and they made their way to the seats at the edge of the dance floor.

Dorothy watched as he got himself a pint and chatted to his mates. He looked confident but somehow vulnerable and she couldn't believe it when he started to walk over to where they were sitting. 'Please let it be me,' she thought as he approached the table and placed his pint in front of them.

"Nice to meet you," he said as he shook her hand, "I'm Cyril."

"Dorothy, and this is Joan."

"Nice to meet you Dorothy and Joan. If you don't mind me saying, you Manchester girls are much nicer looking than the ones in Stoke."

Dorothy blushed and giggled, nudging Joan's arm as if to say, 'here he is, that handsome stranger I was talking about,' but Joan didn't look happy at all.

"What do you for a living Cyril, apart from fall out of coaches with your mates?" asked Joan.

"Well, I'm from Stoke, The Potteries, so I'm the one that makes those delicate tea cups you spend so long drinking from."

"Ha," said Joan, "chance would be a fine thing."

"We're machinists," said Dorothy, "we're the ones that make the shirts you wear when you go out to woo the ladies."

"Ha," said Cyril, "chance would be a fine thing."

Dorothy laughed, but Joan remained stony-faced.

"However, I'm going to break the habit of a life time, just to tell you how lovely you look."

He took Dorothy's hand and kissed it, standing back to admire her and continue with the compliments. Dorothy beamed as he told her what a nice smile she had, how her outfit flattered her figure and how she was a 'looker'. Then; "come on, let's have a dance," he said as he led the way to the floor which throbbed with the heat and rhythm of young bodies out to forget the week's toils.

He was a good mover, easy and natural but with a manly, strong grip. All in all, a fatal combination of good looks, great moves and a charm offensive that would knock the smirk off any rival's face. She didn't stand a chance. They danced for the next half an hour, flirting and chatting, forgetting everything else, including Joan.

"You've a neat little figure on you," he said as he twirled her once, then twice, controlling the dance as he guided her round for a third time then held her securely round her tiny waist.

"Thanks," said Dorothy, not really knowing what else to say, not being accustomed to compliments.

They danced some more until, exhausted with the moves and first meeting nerves, they slumped into the chairs lining the side of the dance floor, glad for a breather. Dorothy spotted Joan looking over at them with an expression which she couldn't fathom. Whatever it was, it wasn't friendly warmth.

'Just like the Mona bleeding Lisa,' thought Dorothy as she lifted her left hand in a wave and smiled, beckoning Joan to join them and feeling slightly guilty for leaving her alone for so long. Joan looked straight through her, then turned on her heels and made her way to the bar.

"She doesn't look right pleased with me," Dorothy commented to Cyril.

"Aye, well she knows what a catch you've got," said Cyril, winking, his eyes twinkling in the light. Then, "listen," he said, "I should really go and have a few with me mates, but I've really enjoyed the dancing tonight."

"Me too," said Dorothy feeling uncertain of what she should do next; go back to Joan or wait for Cyril to arrange another meeting. As she stood, looking to the floor awkwardly and straightening her skirt, Cyril gently lifted her chin.

"Will I see you again?" he asked. Dorothy froze and bit on her lip trying to stop the blush that was rising from her neck upwards.

"Yes, if you want," she said, "but you live quite far away, don't you?"

"Aye well there's always the train," said Cyril, "what about I meet you next Saturday in Manchester, about twelve O" Clock?"

"Yes, why not?" said Dorothy "we could meet outside Woolworths, you can't miss it."

"Grand," said Cyril, "see you outside Woolies at twelve then."

She wished she could get on the coach with him later, be whisked off into the night instead of having to face the wrath of her mother, who she was sure cursed the day she was born. She looked up and smiled nervously.

"Grand," she said, "it's a date."

Then he gave her a quick peck on the cheek and headed back towards the main entrance where she'd first caught sight of him. She saw Joan standing alone by the bar and she made her way over, hoping the backlash wouldn't be too bad. When she was sure he was out of view she did an excited little jig and gripped Joan's hand.

"Well, are you seeing him again?" asked Joan.

"He's meeting me in town next Saturday, can't wait! Isn't he just a dream?"

"Yeah, he's all right" said Joan.

"I think he's the best-looking man I've ever seen," Dorothy replied dreamily but, from the look on Joan's face, she could see that she didn't agree.

For the following week, Dorothy was distracted and could think of nothing else but meeting Cyril on the Saturday. She didn't tell her mum for fear that she'd try to somehow stop the meeting, jeopardise her happiness as she always had. Like the time Dorothy had asked if she could go to college.

"What's the point in that?" her mother had asked.

"So that I can be a teacher," replied Dorothy.

"A teacher? What can you teach anyone? You can't even boil an egg, so no, you can't go to soddin' college, you can go to work like everyone else and bring some money home."

Dorothy could predict how her mother would react to the news that she'd met someone at the dance; 'did he have a white stick? Does he know you can't cook?' So she didn't tell her mother anything.

She couldn't keep it from her dad though, but then her dad had always been fair and understanding. She felt sorry for him, for the life he had with her mum.

He worked so hard, not just at his job, but at trying to

keep her mum happy. She just seemed to make a career out of being miserable and dragging everyone around her down. Sometimes, she would lie in bed all day, shouting down for meals and kicking up a fuss when they didn't arrive quickly enough. Dorothy had heard people refer to her mother as unbalanced or mentally unstable. Others had called her mad, vindictive or controlling. Dorothy had given up trying to get any level of love, respect or even acknowledgement from her, so she just tried to get through each day until she could leave and make some sort of life for herself.

Predictably, her dad had looked happy when she told him about Cyril, although she thought she could also detect a glimmer of disappointment in his eyes, just for a second, then it was gone and he beamed his lovely smile and said how glad he was that she had a young man who could take her out.

"Cyril might just be my saviour, dad; take me off into the sunset to start a new life beyond the factories and the muck."

"Aye, well can I come with you then?" he'd asked jokingly.

But, as he cast his eyes upwards towards the ceiling, towards their bedroom, she thought she sensed a desperation about him; 'Please be happy Dorothy, not like me. Get out of here and make something of your life.'

Dorothy trudged up the narrow staircase with her mother's tea, hoping it might be one of the last times she had to tolerate this trip up to her parents' room which was musty with damp and discontent.

Saturday came and Dorothy's hand shook as she

tried to put on mascara. Today, of all days, she seemed to notice every blemish, every imperfection. She got out her powder compact for the second time and patted away, trying to achieve some semblance of beauty. Once again, the cupid's bow was formed, the same words going through her head 'do I look like a floozy?' She looked long and hard at herself in the mirror and hoped she'd done a good enough job. 'That's if he turns up,' she thought, as she gathered her coat and handbag, looking back to see if her skirt was straight. She caught sight of her sister peeping around the door.

"Hey up our kid, do I look alright?"

"You look lovely, as usual," she replied.

"Aye, well I'm on a date with me very own Prince Charming, but don't tell me mam else she'll have a fit."

Her sister looked her up and down, "Well, if he doesn't fall for you looking like that our kid, he wants his head testing. You're the best-looking girl in Gorton."

"Aw thanks poppet. Here, have this for some sweets, but don't let me mam know else she'll have it off you, more than likely."

"Thank you! I better go to the shop before it shuts for dinner."

"Well hurry up before she knows what you're up to. You can come out with me and sneak back in once you've been. Come on, let's go."

"I'm going now mam," said Dorothy as she stepped around the kitchen door.

"Where are you off to dressed like a prize tart?" came the response.

"I'm going to meet Joan" she said through gritted teeth

as she stepped back around the door. "I'll see you later, I won't need any tea, I'll get something in town."

"The only thing you'll get in town me lady is a nasty disease, looking like you do, and make no mistake."

'Charming,' thought Dorothy. Then she closed the door firmly on what she viewed as the obstacle to all happiness. She raised her brows to her sister and, once the door was shut, did a two-fingered dance, away from her mother's critical glare. She might not be able to see it, but she knew exactly the expression her mother would be wearing, the sour frown that her features settled into by default. She grabbed her sister's hand and, stifling their giggles, they slipped out into the light of a perfect day.

Dorothy felt unsteady as she stepped off the bus at Piccadilly, lost her balance slightly and stumbled a little sideways on the pavement. 'Christ,' she thought, 'anyone'd think I've been on the sherry.' She tried to compose herself but her mind raced, her hands shook and her feet seemed to move slowly and heavily. She stopped by Woolworth's window and squinted, tried to see if she still looked half decent. Then she felt a tap, well, more like a dig on her shoulder and she spun round to see Cyril smiling down at her like one of those cherubs you see on the walls in churches.

"Oh, you made me jump," she said, as she tried to regain control of her lips which were quivering with nerves.

"You look lovely" said Cyril, "I thought we might go to the flicks if you want."

"Yes, that'd be nice," said Dorothy trying to keep calm.

They talked about the kind of week they'd had, Dorothy looking up at him, taking in his features, especially the dark wave of hair arranged so perfectly down to one side. She couldn't believe she was stepping out with such a good-looking man. She hoped he liked her too. He said she looked nice, that had to mean something. He seemed quiet though, distant, as if he had something on his mind. Either that or he didn't want to be there. 'Don't be daft,' she told herself, 'he came all this way on the train, didn't he?'

"Do you have brothers and sisters at home?" she managed to ask, thinking, too late, how uninventive the question was.

"Yeah, just the four, two boys eighteen and twelve and two girls fifteen and four."

"That's quite a big family then," she said and "there's just three of us, me and my sister, she's sixteen and I've an older brother, he's twenty-one."

"Right," he said looking disinterested, Dorothy thought.

Then he turned to look at her, flashed that crooked smile and she was trapped in his gaze. She hoped he couldn't see the blush rising from her chest and burning her face. She was trying to be as calm as he was.

There was an awkward moment as they arrived at the picture house. She wasn't used to dating, as such, so she wasn't sure whether to offer to pay for her own ticket. She started to rummage in her handbag but Cyril firmly put his hand on hers.

"I'll get this," he said as he squeezed the life out of her tiny fist.

"Oh right, thanks," Dorothy stuttered, but she felt

uncomfortable. 'Was that a warning?' she wondered. He had squeezed her hand so hard, the knuckles had cracked. 'No,' she thought, 'it was just him showing affection, he doesn't know his own strength.'

Tickets and sweets were bought and she followed Cyril into the darkness of the cinema, trying to avoid any further awkward moments. She let him choose where to sit, didn't want him to think her too forward for choosing the back row. They climbed the central stairs right to the top and he winked as he edged his way into the middle of the very back seats. He chose a double Pullman and they settled down against the velvet, Cyril arranging his arm around her shoulder. It felt good, she felt warm, wanted and excited. That was when Cyril moved in for the first kiss. It wasn't tender, as she'd expected, but urgent. He almost bit and bruised her lip and she had to pull away for air. She couldn't read the expression on his face. Hurt or anger? His eyes were black and unreadable, so she stared straight ahead at the screen, fearful that she might cry and spoil everything. Cyril put his hand on her knee, then took her hand, this time more gently, not as urgently and they shuffled back to watch the film.

Dorothy thought that Cyril must have felt just as awkward as she did, hence his clumsiness. Once she had dispelled her doubts, she could relax, but if anyone had asked her what the film was about, she would have struggled to answer them.

The rest of the date was uneventful; they arranged to meet again, the following week, then she waved him off at the station and made her way home.

On the third date, after the pub and before the train home, Cyril suggested that they walk through the park as it would be better than walking through the 'shitty streets of Gorton.' It was dark and the park gates were closed, but they found a gap and squeezed in. She giggled, but when she looked at Cyril he wasn't smiling. She couldn't read his expression, but he stared at her intently, then he took her hand roughly and lead her into a grassed area behind some bushes. He sat on the ground, then pulled her down next to him where she landed with a thud. It was frosty and she shrieked with the shock of the cold ground touching her legs.

"Hush," he said, "Someone might hear us and tell us to clear off."

Then he straddled her, kissing her hard on the lips, pushing her breast with one hand and trying to part her thighs with the other. She was terrified, unable to move or speak, only just managing to breathe between each assault on her mouth. Her skirt was tight and he used both hands to yank it up to her waist, ripping the seams, and all without looking at her, without speaking and all she could do was freeze into the frozen ground and bite her tongue to stop the tears. He roughly pulled at her underwear, ripping her nylons and pulling her knickers down over her knees which would have knocked, had they been together. She was frightened, and when he released himself, she couldn't help but let out a gasp as he forced himself onto her.

"That's right, you want it too, don't you?"

But she didn't and nothing could prepare her for the searing pain as he entered her and she groaned then and he covered her mouth as he gyrated and pushed and pushed, only stopping when he had spurted into her. He let out a sound of pleasure, then rolled off, leaning back on his elbows to get his breath back. He turned and winked at her, then bent down to retrieve his underwear from around his ankles. Now it was his turn to gasp.

"Shite, Dorothy, you didn't tell me you were on."

"I'm not, what do you mean?"

She sat up and looked down at the bloody mess, ashamed of what she'd done. She found a hankie in her handbag, quickly wiped herself, wincing as she did. She was cut and bruised and this was not how she had imagined it would be. She sobbed and pulled on her underwear, trying to hide her mood from him in case he thought she was just a stupid kid. Her nylons were unsalvageable, so she rolled them into a ball and threw them under the hedge, hoping her mother would be in bed when she got home. Thankfully, her skirt was around her waist, so hadn't been bloodied. She pulled it down. It was crumpled and torn, like her, not quite what it had been at the beginning of this awful night.

"I'm sorry," he said, not looking her in the eye, "I didn't know like, didn't think anyone your age still was, you know, a virgin."

"Aye, well I'm not, now am I? Anyway, it doesn't matter, it had to happen sooner or later, didn't it?"

"I would have been more careful if I'd have known, you know."

"Yeah, I know."

But she didn't know, she didn't know at all. She didn't know anything about life, about men, about how you were supposed to behave. She had only really known one man and that was her father. Was he like this? Is this what it was like for them? She couldn't imagine it. She stood up, looked at her outline in the frost, like a murder scene.

"I'll walk you home before I get my train," he said, following her, grabbing her hand and walking beside her out of the park, down the back streets and to her door where he kissed her briefly, said a quick 'goodnight,' then disappeared into the evening fog.

Dorothy mouthed a quick prayer, her hand shaking as she tried to engage her key in the lock. Just as she managed, her father pulled the door open and she fell into him. She held him around the neck and cried for a long time, her body convulsing with sobs until she was spent. He held her and when she dared to look up, she saw a single tear escape and trickle down his right cheek. That's when she knew that all men were not the same, that her dad was one of the good ones.

"Is that Dorothy?" her mother roared from on high.

"Yes, it is, she's in now, she's going to bed."

He led her up to her room and gently closed the door, leaving her with her confusion and shame. It was true, she knew nothing about men and life and how you should behave, but she didn't want to find out this way. For a time, she sat on a towel on the edge of her bed, as frozen as she was earlier on the frosty ground. Then she used a warm flannel to wash her stinging parts and found clean underwear to cover them. She pulled on the longest flannelette nightdress she could find and she crawled into bed, hugging her knees for comfort. After a couple of hours of fitful tossing and turning of both body and mind, she cried herself to sleep, her head aching as if it were in the grip of a vice and that song going around in a loop in her mind.

Despite the pain and confusion of their first sexual encounter, Dorothy had agreed to see Cyril again, charmed by his excuses and explanations. She saw him every weekend and, as they got to know each other more, there was no doubt in Dorothy's mind that he could be 'the one'. Meeting him was the highlight of her week and her thoughts revolved around what to wear and where they'd go. Afterwards, she'd analyse each word and look until she thought she'd go mad with all the thinking. She hardly dared to speculate whether he loved her, but she hoped that he might, just a little bit. The trouble was, Cyril was so hard to read. Whenever he looked her straight in the eye, she didn't know if it was hatred or lust behind that cool stare of his. She didn't know whether to gloat or to fear for her life.

The next few months went by in a blur of meetings with Cyril, trying to ignore her mother's insults and working at the factory where she sat, humped over a machine all day, sewing garments.

Meanwhile, her friendship with Joan had been tested to the limit as Dorothy became more engrossed in her relationship with Cyril. She'd noticed that Joan had become quite sullen and seemed to completely switch off when Cyril was mentioned. Once, when she was telling her about a date they'd been on, Joan asked, 'What are you bothering with him for? Anyone can see he's not good for you.' Dorothy had asked what she meant, but Joan just shook her head and gave her a look of pity. Dorothy put it all down to jealousy, especially as Joan hadn't met anyone yet. They still went out occasionally, but Joan kept saying it wasn't the same now Dorothy was 'mooning around like a lovesick fool.' Despite the tension in their relationship, Joan was still the first person, the only person Dorothy called on if she needed to talk. She spoke to her about everything, but most of all about 'women's things'. Her mother was hard and far from interested, positively discouraged Dorothy from coming to her with any problems or worries. However, she hadn't felt able to talk, even to Joan, about that night with Cyril.

Now, she stood on Joan's doorstep, her heart heavy with fear, regret and apprehension and her mind full of scenarios waiting to be aired and ironed out. She lifted the brass knocker and rapped a couple of times half-heartedly, as if she wasn't sure she wanted Joan to appear or not. The news she brought could be the final hammer-blow to a relationship which had endured childish fallouts, teenage jealousies and the Second World War.

She could hear Joan's footsteps down the hall, bare floorboards allowing the sound to filter through the barrier of the door and into Dorothy's consciousness. She straightened herself and drew a deep breath in anticipation of the unburdening that lay immediately ahead and the repercussions a little further along the way. The sound of the latch being lifted and the clunk as its mechanism released and allowed the barrier to be pulled slightly open jolted Dorothy further from her daydreams. Joan's face appeared through the gap like a luminous moon gliding ominously from the cover of cloud to bring light, but light heavy with consequence.

"Hiya kid," Dorothy said, in a futile attempt to keep the tone light.

"I was just going to bed," said Joan, even though Dorothy could see that, clearly, she wasn't, as she was wearing her pill box hat, perched on one side of her head as if to mock the imposter who had dared to step foot on her threshold.

"I've something to tell you," said Dorothy, "it's important."

"Right, well you'd better come in for a minute," said Joan, opening the door slowly as Dorothy stepped into the breach. She followed Joan up the stairs, careful not to slip on the threadbare runner or the clips which held it in place. She had a feeling that a great metaphorical door was closing in on her, shutting her out, denying her the luxury of a confidante. Who could she turn to now? Who would listen when she really needed someone to share her thoughts with, woman-to-woman. Certainly not her mother. 'Christ,' thought Dorothy 'I suppose I'd better tell her next.' As Joan slowly pushed open the door to her bedroom, she suddenly spun round and faced Dorothy with a contemptuous look laden with something bordering, Dorothy thought, on hatred.

"Don't tell me, please for the love of God, don't tell me you're pregnant."

The tears fell now, and rolled down cheeks flushed with self-pity as Dorothy realised in that instant that she had lost her good friend, probably forever.

"It's not what you think, Joan, we were careful!"

"Careful? You don't get pregnant by being careful, Dorothy."

Dorothy followed Joan and plonked herself on the edge of her bed, Joan pacing the room, impatient to be somewhere else.

"I've not got long, I'm going out in a minute."

"I thought you might be. I didn't know who else I could talk to Joan, you know what me mam's like".

"Well you're going to have to tell her sooner or later."

"I know, but I wanted to work things out first, before I go blurting it out to me mam and dad."

Dorothy waited for Joan's response, but she just stood there looking at her in disbelief.

"I want to see what Cyril thinks first, before I tell anyone else."

"What Cyril thinks? I can probably tell you what Cyril thinks, that he's sorry he ever met you, getting into trouble like this. I can bet he isn't the settling down type."

"You don't know him Joan, he treats me right, you know."

"Well, obviously he doesn't, or else you wouldn't be in this mess."

Dorothy realised the futility of the visit. She wasn't going to get any reassurance from Joan, if anything, she felt worse than ever.

"Well, I'd better go. I hope you have a nice night out."

"Thanks. I hope you sort it out, whatever you decide to do."

Joan pushed open the bedroom door, then followed Dorothy down the stairs. Dorothy waited at the bottom, but when Joan reached her, she walked past and opened the front door, holding it so that Dorothy could go out first. She didn't offer her friend a hug or any kind words, so Dorothy lifted her hand in a half-hearted wave and walked away. When she looked back, Joan was half-running in the opposite direction, eager to continue with the rest of the evening. 'How did we get to this?' thought Dorothy, but she knew. She had neglected her friend in favour of a man. She hadn't listened to advice and now she was on her own.

Later, when she thought about it, she realised that Joan hadn't smiled once during the whole conversation, couldn't wait for it to be over, so that she could resume her own life. Dorothy had always known how important her best friend was. She had been with her though life's saddest and happiest times, held her hand and wiped away tears. She'd loaned her perfume and mascara, even money, until pay day. She'd advised her on clothes, jobs and boys. That didn't matter now, all that mattered was breaking the news to Cyril and the hope that he would be pleased, because that was her only hope.

Dorothy put off going to the doctor's until she was quite sure and when the time came, she sat nervously at the end of a row of chairs, hoping nobody would see her.

Then, "Dorothy Atkins," she heard through the buzz of her thoughts and it made her jump. She stood and walked falteringly to the doctor's imposing wooden door. 'Shine a light,' she thought, 'here we go.' She pushed the door and edged her way into his consulting room, her heart racing. She sat down and clung onto her handbag as if he wasn't a doctor at all, but a bandit waiting to rob her of all she possessed.

Doctor Fraser looked at her with that same unreadable expression he always wore and asked, "what brings you here today, young lady?"

"I think I'm pregnant," she replied, bowing her head and trying to look sombre but not quite managing to stop the corners of her mouth turning upwards slightly.

He looked at her intently and said, "remind me of your age."

"I'm eighteen," she said fumbling with the edge of her jacket.

"And the father, is he around? Do you intend to get married?"

"Oh, yes, he is and yes we do," she replied, crossing her fingers behind her back.

"Right, well I suppose congratulations are in order then young miss. Take this bottle and bring us a sample of urine. We'll do the test and see you in two weeks' time."

Dorothy took the container, her hand shaking as she did so. She slipped it into her bag, got up and said, "thank you" as she left the room. The doctor's visit had made everything seem real now and she walked home in a daze. She slipped her hand through the gap between the buttons on her coat and rested it lightly on her stomach. She felt warm, satisfied, but vulnerable. She had yet to tell her parents the news, then there was Cyril. She could deal with her parents, because it wouldn't be long before she left, if all went to plan. It was Cyril's reaction that worried her the most, because it was key to how her future would develop. If he said he wanted nothing to do with her or the baby, what would happen to her? It would bring shame on the family and she'd probably have to go away and have it adopted, then come back and pretend nothing had happened. Her mother would make her life even more miserable than it is now and her father would be disappointed. She could only hope that her fears were unfounded, that Cyril would be pleased, because the alternative was too much to bear. She had the daydream, but when she thought about it rationally, she didn't know

Cyril at all, not really. They hadn't been seeing each other that long, but had become closer, if you can call it that, in the last few weeks. The intimacy had improved since that brutal first time and they were getting along fine. She thought so, anyway.

Once she told Cyril, she would have to tell her parents and she wasn't looking forward to that at all. She arrived home and came hurtling back to the present as she gingerly opened the front door and stepped inside the house. She walked through to the kitchen where her mother was sitting on a wooden stool by the fire. Well, not so much sitting as spilling over it, her generous proportions seeming to fill the room, leaving no space for anything else. With her legs open, but her modesty preserved by the layers of her undergarments and full cotton skirts, she shuffled on the stool, glared at Dorothy and asked,

"What are you looking so pleased about? And where've you been 'til this time? Your tea's been ready nearly half an hour."

"Nowhere," replied Dorothy, "I mean, I just called in at Joan's for a brew after work. Sorry Mam, I never thought."

"No, you never 'think' do you? That's why you're gonna spend the rest of your days in that factory 'til you get yourself knocked up by some poor sod too blind to see how useless you are."

Dorothy hung her head and shuffled towards the stove, wondering how her mother always managed to be so astute, always knew what to say to make her feel dreadful. She took the warm plates out of the oven and carried them over to the little wooden table.

"Thanks for tea Mam," she said, trying to conceal her hurt. She lifted the top plate off to reveal a dried-up portion of Shepherd's pie.

"It's your Dad you've to thank," her mother said, "he's the one daft enough to cook for a little mare who doesn't deserve it. And what's this letter 'ere on the mantel piece? Eh? Who're you cavorting with from Stoke?"

Dorothy ate slowly, nearly choking on the meal and the atmosphere, which was thick with tension and resentment. She gazed surreptitiously at the letter propped up on the shelf and speculated about its content. He hadn't said the words yet, so maybe this was his way of telling her how he felt. She knew he was quite shy and awkward about things like that and the more she thought about it, the more she convinced herself that the letter contained a declaration of love. She glowed with the thought of it. She finished eating, washed up under the oppressive glare of her mother and took the letter up to her room, cherishing the feel of it. She slumped on the edge of the bed and slipped off her shoes, rolled her stockings down and removed them carefully. Her hand settled on her stomach as she tried to steady her breathing. She picked up the envelope and studied the writing and the post mark. 'My Cyril,' she thought as she slipped her thumb along the gummed flap that sealed his words.

Dear Dorothy,

I am having to sort out some problems at home so I won't be able to see you for a couple of weeks.

It's me Mam. She's not very well, no thanks to me Dad and I've to look after the others 'til she gets better.

Cyril.

Dorothy's heart sank. 'No kiss at the end,' she thought, 'so much for a declaration of love.' Her hand dropped limply to the bed and the letter crumpled under it. The disappointment hit her hard. She thought about the brevity of the note, not a letter after all, and certainly not a declaration of love. She convinced herself that he didn't even care about her, let alone love her. Everything was pointing that way and there wasn't a thing she could do about it. 'Why did this have to happen now?' she thought, 'just when I'm starting to get my miserable little life sorted out.'

She felt guilty and selfish for thinking what bad timing it was. She felt heavy with the disappointment of not seeing Cyril for a while. Now she'd have to keep her news of the baby buried until she saw him again, if she saw him again. 'I bloody hate life,' she thought as the tears escaped and dropped onto the crumpled letter. Her pathetic frame convulsed with the pain of it all, a culmination of years of feeling unworthy and unloved wracked her body and she shuddered, rattling the iron bed frame. When the tears finally stopped, she felt numb, then she remembered the baby. 'Pull yourself together, you daft cow,' she thought, as she unfolded herself slowly and looked at her image in the dressing table mirror. 'What a mess,' she thought, 'What a bloody mess. I mean, look at me. My hair's thin and limp, I look tired and haggard and I can't even think straight. Why would anyone want me?'

For the following week or so, Dorothy's emotions soared and dipped and never seemed to settle into any semblance of calm. The lows of disappointment and emptiness seemed to dominate her general mood, but then she would become overwhelmed by bliss at the thought of having Cyril's child and setting up home with him. Dorothy tried to keep herself together and function as normally as possible so she could at least get through each day at work. 'Just sit it out,' she told herself after she'd recovered from the impact of the letter. 'Don't ruin your chances by making a fuss, just let him do what he's got to do and then tell him the news and hope for the best,' she thought and 'you never know, he might be just as keen to escape as I am.'

When she finally met up with Cyril again after three weeks, she was at least armed with the results of the test. Yes, she was pregnant and she was weary from thinking and over-thinking. She was struggling to keep a lid on the feelings and thoughts that swam around her mind. That song was back, going round and round in a loop in her head. Her emotions and words competed like voices in a choir wanting to be heard. She tried to control them, hold them back and calm them into a kind of harmony while she found the right way to tell him. It was important that she didn't just blurt it out; her future depended on it. She certainly didn't want to come across as uncaring, because after all, he had his own problems at home, which he would probably want to tell her about in more detail.

They were sitting in a little back street café waiting for their order when she reached for his hand over the Formica table. She was trying to gauge his mood but he wasn't giving much away. He didn't even seem pleased to see her and this made her feel uneasy. He seemed a bit sullen, if truth be known and Dorothy tried to convince herself that this had nothing to do with her, more to do with his situation at home.

"So, how've you been then, how are things at home?" she asked now, holding on to his fingers and trying to stroke him back to her.

"Oh er, all right, you know, all right," he replied, withdrawing his hand and picking up the menu.

Dorothy tried to keep her thoughts reasonable but she struggled and was almost in tears when the hand was pulled away from the affection she offered.

"Oh good, I'm glad things are better at home," she managed, withdrawing her own hand now and looking down into her lap so he might not see the tears brimming.

"Are you alright?" he asked and there was such a lack of feeling that Dorothy finally broke and allowed the words, which had simmered for so long, to come tumbling out randomly.

"No, I'm not really. I'm going to have a baby if you must know and it's just been so bloody awful these last few weeks, not being able to tell anyone, not me mam, not me dad, not you and now it seems like you don't want to know and, God what a mess, what a bloody, stupid rotten mess." She slumped into her own body, gave in to the despair.

"Well aren't you going to say something?" she said through sobs which made her gasp for breath every couple of words.

"Jesus, Dorothy," he said at last, "what do you want me to say? Do you think I came here today expecting this? Me minds buggered up enough as it is with what's happened at home without having to deal with this as well."

"Well, you better bloody had deal with it," she blurted,

just as two plates were put down between them causing them both to sit up and push back from the table as they tried to pull themselves back to normality.

"We'd better eat this, since it's here," said Cyril, picking up his cutlery and looking down at the plate in front of him.

"How can you think about sodding egg and chips after what I've just told you?" she asked.

"Because I'm starving, that's why. I haven't eaten since I got on the train to come and see you, so you can please yourself, but I'm having mine," he said as he speared the first chip and thrust it down into the egg, breaking its membrane so the yolk spilled over onto the plate.

Dorothy didn't think she'd ever felt so wretched and defeated, for all she'd been through at home. All the put-downs and sneered insults that she'd endured throughout her life seemed to pale now with this fresh hurt.

She watched as Cyril ate ravenously, apparently oblivious to her pain and she wondered how things could ever be good after this. She sat, like the wallflower at the end of a dance, alone and not wanting anyone to see her for the shame of it.

After what seemed like a lifetime, Cyril cleaned the congealing egg yolk from around his plate with the last of the bread then wiped his mouth with the back of his hand and looked intently at Dorothy who couldn't hold his gaze.

"So, what do we do now then?" he asked, his voice shaking with the anger and injustice of being landed with such heavy news so soon. "I hardly know you and now we're having to sort this out. As if I haven't enough to think about with me Mam an' all. Now, I've something to tell you Dorothy. Something so bad, I haven't got my own head around it yet."

It was Cyril's turn to hang his head while he searched for words. Dorothy, once again, reached for his hand and, once again, he withdrew. She stared at him wide-eyed, not knowing what to expect.

Cyril inhaled deeply, still looking down. "There's no good way of saying this, so I'll just say it how it is. My mam and dad had a massive row last Sunday, something to do with him being seen with another woman, I don't really know. Anyway, my dad got that mad, he got hold of my mam's hair like, and he dragged her round the garden, kicking her all the time, with her pleading for him to stop an' all. By the time I got out, she was in a bad way. The ambulance came, but we got news later that she couldn't be saved and neither could the baby. I didn't even know she was pregnant. Now I've got no mam and my dad's banged up and I've got four kids there to think about. Then you tell me this, Christ!"

Dorothy reeled with the shock of it, searched the turmoil for something to say, but each phrase that formulated seemed futile. Her throat was so thick, she doubted if she could speak anyway.

"Well, it's no use just sitting there is it? What do you want me to do, just leave you here and go back home on the train, let you sort it out yourself?"

"No" she managed to rasp and "I don't know what to say, what to do."

Once again, she felt like the charmless, stupid kid

that nobody wanted to bother with. She didn't have the confidence to speak again, so she left it to Cyril.

They would have to get married he said, "No kid of mine is going to be raised without a father," was his reasoning. He would find work in Manchester and they would have to rent a little house somewhere cheap. The kids were staying with their aunty and uncle for now, so they'd have to stay there until things were sorted out.

Dorothy swallowed and her throat felt a bit easier now. She managed to look at him and hope he wasn't repulsed by what he saw, the state of her.

"I'm sorry," she whispered, "I didn't want it to be like this."

"Well, we'll just have to make the most of it won't we, sort it out and get on with it," he said.

Dorothy was relieved at the shift from anger in Cyril's tone to a sort of resigned acceptance. They stood and faced each other, seemingly unsure of what to do next. Then Dorothy shuffled slowly round the table and slipped her hand into his.

"We'll be all right," she said, without any degree of certainty at all.

CHAPTER 4

Marriage, Birth and Decline

1949

The wedding was a small affair, with a reception held in the back room of one of the local pubs. Sandwiches, pork pies, port and lemon, brown ale and each family weighing up the other for suitability. As it happens, they were quite evenly matched if you looked at social bearing. Neither family was in the gutter, nor had they reached the heady heights of being labelled middle-class. They worked hard in menial jobs, trying to feed their families and getting by with a 'make do and mend' philosophy. Neighbours played an important, supportive role in times of need. They looked out for each other, minded each other's children, gave loans of bread, sugar, butter, whatever was short until payday. They handed down clothes that no longer fit, gave advice and listened to troubles. The only thing they didn't have to give was money. Times were hard, especially if you had a large family to feed.

Dorothy sat in the dark corner of the 'snug' and looked around at the happy scene of the two families sharing food, drink, jokes and anecdotes. The strain of the last couple of months had taken its toll and, although she was over the initial bout of morning sickness, she still felt weary. The wedding had been a rush to organise but had served as a tool with which to appease her mother after the news of the baby. Dorothy braced herself through the 'I told you so', 'It's your bed, lie in it', 'stupid girl' talks and, eventually, her mother resigned herself to the news and even helped to arrange the registry office, flowers and cake.

Dorothy wasn't sure what lay ahead but was certain it could only be an improvement on what went before. No more of her mother's disapproving looks and put-downs. No more sneaking around and worrying about what her mother would say when she got in. She was looking forward to starting married life with Cyril in the house they had managed to rent in Winton. It was only small but the area was decent. It was a start and, what's more, it was away from the daily glare of her mother; a bus and a train ride away to be precise. She knew things wouldn't be easy, as she'd have to give up her job as a machinist soon, which would mean living off one income. That was going to be a strain, but it was already getting difficult to get close enough to the machine and the days were long and physically exhausting. At the end of a working day, her neck ached with the strain of bending over the machine and pushing through garment after garment from a never-ending pile. Her fingers were dry, red and sore and, when she sat hunched over her work, the heartburn now was almost unbearable. It was difficult to get time away from her workbench as every visit to the toilet was monitored and timed. Anything over a certain amount was docked from her wages and she needed every penny while she could still earn. Pregnancy was certainly not a reason to be more generous with breaks, so Dorothy had to grit her teeth and carry on until she could no longer bear it.

Cyril had managed to find work as a furniture salesman in a shop just around the corner. He had charmed the owner, as Dorothy knew he would and, despite his lack of experience, they took a chance on him. He had wasted no time becoming friendly with the other workers and joining them for drinks. Already, he had become a familiar face in the local and was considered a 'regular'. He had also befriended some of the other regulars, which didn't surprise Dorothy as, despite her early experiences of him, she couldn't deny that he was quite the social charmer. It seemed that she wasn't the only one to be taken in by that handsome grin and easy wit. It wasn't just the ladies who fell for it either, men were just as impressed by his worldly knowledge and his ability to tell a yarn or two. Wherever he went, you could see that people around him were in awe of this easy entertainer, beguiled by his story-telling and taken in by his charm.

They had known each other less than a year and had only just begun to feel comfortable as a couple. Dorothy looked forward to a time when she could feel secure, even complacent with Cyril and she wondered how long it would be before she could wave him off at the door and be sure that he was going to return. She didn't know if her doubts stemmed from her own upbringing or just from the fact that he was so bloody handsome and, like the Pied Piper, had people following as he played his enchanting tune. Either way, she would torture herself with thoughts of him chatting up other women while out at the pub. She would wonder how many, on any given night, had been smitten by his good looks and easy charm, just as she had been. She hoped the wedding ring would deter any future would-be admirers and serve as a reminder to Cyril of his responsibilities. Looking at his handsome profile, she felt lucky to call him her husband, but cursed at the same time. She let out a sigh and immediately felt a dig in her side.

Her mother, still stern, even on her daughter's wedding day, sat resolute in her martyrdom and misery. To Dorothy, she looked like the gargoyles on old buildings, her stony features set in the most unattractive look of contempt you could imagine. She gave Dorothy one such look now,

"I thought your wedding day were supposed to be happiest day of your life. You look like you've just lost a pound and found thrippence."

"I am happy Mam, I was just thinking, that's all."

"Aye well, thinking won't put clothes on the back of the child, will it? "

"No Mam, I don't suppose it will, but at least I can sew. I can make a lot of my own clothes and I'm sure I'll be able to knock up a few baby clothes when the time comes."

Her mother looked at her as if she were mad. 'Putting clothes on the baby's back' is a saying. It means earning enough to keep your family! How do you think the pair of you are going to do that, eh? God knows, *we* struggle, and you father's twice the man Cyril will ever be."

Dorothy wondered why her mother could not give her a reprieve, especially on her wedding day. "We can only try our best, can't we? And that's what we'll do, our best."

Dorothy stood up and walked slowly away from the woman who had caused her so much misery and seemed intent on causing more. She joined Cyril and caught the tail-end of a taunt from one of his friends, about an end to his womanising days. This didn't help Dorothy's state of mind at all and she pursed her lips as she tried to smile and stem the tears at the same time. She knew she had to stop being so sensitive. Maybe it was the pregnancy.

"We were just telling Cyril how lucky he is to have such a beautiful woman for a wife," said the one who had taunted.

Dorothy smiled tightly and held Cyril's hand, looking forward to when they could escape the party and be alone. She felt him stumble slightly and realised he must have had a few pints. 'Oh well,' she reasoned, 'it is our wedding day, he's allowed to get merry today of all days.' She stood a while longer, waiting to be included in the conversation but too nervous to join in. She watched Cyril and his mates as they laughed, staggered and knocked back beer. She tried to talk, but was largely ignored and, what had started as harmless banter, had now deteriorated into smutty jokes and tales of past conquests. Dorothy slipped away, seemingly unnoticed. She went to join her sister who was perched on a bar stool looking glum. Dorothy was sure that her own misery was bigger than her sister's, or anyone else's for that matter, but she felt duty-bound at least to try and cheer up her younger sibling.

"Hey up our kid, what's up, has no one asked you to dance yet?" she asked as she took hold of her sister's hands and pulled her gently off the stool.

"Come on, let's have our last dance before I leave you

to go and live in me little house. You'll have to buy your own lipsticks now, won't you, or nick 'em from Woolies more like."

This made her sister smile slightly and Dorothy's heart lurched as she recognised the same self-conscious uncertainty on the face of her sister, as that which haunted her own features. She gripped her hands, but didn't know what to say or do to save this wretched little soul from enduring the same fate as herself. She wished she could whisk her away from that pit of despair they were supposed to call 'home', but she knew that it would cause too many problems for her and Cyril, so all she could do was to be there whenever she could.

"You know you can always talk to me, don't you? You can come to tea, even stay over sometimes if you want and you can help me look after the baby when it comes."

"I'm going to really miss you Dorothy. I don't know how I'll go on with me mam, now I'm on my own. She's bound to pick on me now that you're not here and I'll have no big sister to run to."

Dorothy's heart was breaking. "Well that's what I've just said, haven't I? I might not be in the same house, but you know you can come around anytime you like."

"I know, but you don't want me there all the time, you've just got married. You don't want your kid sister spoiling it by turning up on your doorstep."

Dorothy knew that her sister was right. She also knew that Cyril would not like it if Rosie were to spend too much time at their house. It was a dilemma.

"Don't worry our kid, it will all turn out good in the end."

She kissed Rosie's cheek and led her over to Aunty Betty, their father's sister, where she left her being fussed over.

It was almost midnight and the last of the revellers were leaving. Cyril was at the bar downing another shot of whisky. Dorothy approached him and slipped her hand in his, looking forward to being carried over the threshold and to them being alone so that they could snuggle up in their marital bed. She gasped as Cyril snatched his hand away with such force that it stung. When she looked up, he was looming over her, his face almost puce and with an expression of pure hatred.

"Don't you come here trying to work your way around me," he spluttered, slurring his words and spitting. "Don't think I didn't notice you sneaking off to dance with your sister and all the men staring at you."

Dorothy felt too helpless and shocked to respond, but managed to make a feeble attempt at defending herself.

"Rosie's sixteen years old and as innocent as they come. I was only trying to cheer her up because she's going to be left on her own with me mam, and you know what she's like."

"Yeah well you didn't have to do it in the middle of the pub did you? You didn't have to dance around like a pair of tarts with all eyes on you. You'd already shown me up when you walked off in front of me mates."

Dorothy was confused and hurt. She had thought she hadn't been welcome in the circle of friends and that he wouldn't have minded her slipping away, would have been glad of it. Now he was in such a rage and she failed to see how something so seemingly minor could have triggered this dark mood. She'd never seen him this angry before and it scared her. She thought about what to say, she thought very carefully because if she said the wrong thing, he could go off like a Roman Candle.

"Can we go now, I'm really tired?" she asked and was relieved when Cyril's tight expression seemed to relax a little and he replied,

"Yeah, well we might as well as there's no one left worth talking to. I've had enough now anyway."

He took her hand roughly as he led her around the room to say goodbye to the few remaining guests. She tried not to let the hurt show in her face and was thankful when, finally, they were on their way home through the dark back streets.

Neither of them had spoken during the walk and Dorothy felt she should break the silence as they reached the front door.

"Sorry if you felt shown up. I just thought you wanted me to leave you to enjoy the banter with your mates."

"Listen, you're married to me now and I'm not having you flirting all over town like some cheap floozy."

Dorothy knew he was drunk and it was no use responding, trying to reason. She put the key in the door and entered what she had come to think of as her little haven.

Cyril stumbled in after her and went straight upstairs to bed. Dorothy locked up and followed him to the bedroom. There he lay, flat on his back, already asleep, stupefied. She let out a frustrated sigh and started to undress. Each garment was reluctantly peeled away and cast aside. She had wanted him to remove her wedding attire. She had wanted him to gasp at her bosom, which was fuller than ever and encased in the prettiest bra she could afford. She had wanted him to be overcome with love and lust when her demure underskirts revealed the white stockings. Instead, she had to remove her own clothes, stifling her sobs as she did so. She had never felt so lonely and, as she snuggled into Cyril, he turned his back on her, making her feel thoroughly wretched.

The night passed slowly, graced by fitful bouts of sleep, disturbing thoughts and Cyril's snoring. She hoped this wasn't a taste of things to come but, deep inside, she knew it probably was and the thought depressed her. When her body finally surrendered to something resembling sleep, she was nudged from her slumber, sharply in the ribs. Not by the child within, but the one without; Cyril demanding tea.

As she awoke, images of her so-called wedding night presented themselves and she groaned as she swung her legs round to the edge of the bed ready to attend to her husband's needs. The thought that it shouldn't be tea he was asking for didn't escape her, and she felt like an undesirable failure. She knew better than to risk reaching out to him though; another rejection now would bring her to tears and she was quite sure that Cyril would be more annoyed if she started to cry.

She swallowed down the hurt and disappointment. "Cup o' tea then?" she asked.

He mumbled something affirmative and she trudged slowly down the narrow stairs; 'Narrow' she thought, 'like the route of my bloody life. What went before, what lies ahead, isn't much different really.'

The stark realisation that this was her lot hit her hard and she slumped on the stairs and sat for a moment to contemplate what, if anything, she could do. She couldn't talk to her mother, she'd be beyond intolerable. Her father had already said how happy he was that she'd found someone who would look after her, so she couldn't talk to him, it would break his heart. Joan had been lost long ago. She would just have to try to appease Cyril somehow and hope this black mood passed quickly. She rose and continued to the kitchen where she prepared tea and what to say next.

It was a nostalgic climb back up the wooden stairs as Dorothy was reminded of the times she took tea up to her mother, with the same heavy heart and sense of dread. The same 'who'd want me?' overpowering and overriding any other thoughts, an equal sense of contempt waiting in the room above ready to smother her as she entered.

It was ironic how her fractured childhood had made her lack self-esteem, but somehow had bestowed her with an amazing sense of calm and strength when it came to tackling life's challenges. She took a deep breath, nudged open the door and smiled down at her husband who was lying on the conjugal bed looking nothing like a vision of desire.

"I've brought your tea," she said as she edged her way on to the bed.

"Oh er, thanks love," he replied and he reached out for her hand. "Look, I'm sorry about last night, I'm an awkward sod when I've had a drink and it's been a tough time, what with the kids and everything."

The grin across Dorothy's face clearly displayed her relief. "I know, I know, but at least they're settled now so let's just forget last night," she said, "give us kiss and I'll forgive you."

Cyril leant up on one elbow, his face on one side still crumpled from sleep, his hair a tousled mess. His eyes were red and puffy and, Dorothy thought, full of remorse. She kissed him tenderly, smoothing back his hair and feeling light with the sense of a burden being lifted. 'Thank God,' she thought, as the focus at last shifted from needing tea to wanting each other. They drew into a hug and laughed as the lump got in the way.

"How's our little Eric anyway?" asked Cyril, as he rested his hand on the ever-increasing mound.

"She's fine thanks," said Dorothy and they continued with their banter about the sex of the baby as they cuddled and kissed their way back to what Dorothy had hoped for, a loving start to married life.

They finally emerged from the marital bed about midday, dressed, then strolled back to The Hare and Hounds to collect the pile of wedding presents and other things they had left behind. The landlord looked up from pulling a pint and raised an eyebrow to them.

"All right this evening, are we?" he asked, directing his gaze at Cyril.

"It's barely twelve o' clock and we're right as rain, thanks" said Dorothy quickly, sensing Cyril's unease.

"Pint o' bitter for me and, what are you having love?"

"Oh, I thought we were just collecting presents and taking them home," she said, noticing how Cyril's face dropped as she did so.

"No harm in having a pint, to celebrate your first day of married life with a lovely woman though is there?"

Dorothy smiled "just an orange juice for me," she said, and "I'll take these home while you drink that." She walked towards the table in the corner which was piled high with gifts and cards, their shiny presence a welcome oasis in the doom of the bar's lounge.

"There's no rush is there?" asked Cyril, as he took her arm and pulled her sharply back to him.

"No, I don't suppose there is," she said and she stood once more, next to her husband at the bar, uncertain of what lay ahead. 'It's like being on the bleeding big dipper,' she secretly thought, while outwardly she turned on the most convincing smile she could muster.

One pint turned into three and Dorothy tried to feel a part of this world, but the truth was, she wasn't comfortable watching Cyril slowly get drunk again. He was at the merry stage now but she knew that could change very quickly. If she suggested they leave, he might get annoyed, but she thought it was worth a try anyway.

"Do you think we should go and get some lunch?" she asked as Cyril lifted his glass to drain the remaining inch of bitter.

He glanced at her sideways with a look she couldn't decipher, slammed his pot down and shouted over for another pint. Humiliated and upset, Dorothy bit her lip and looked down to the floor. After a few seconds, she suggested that she took some of the presents home while he finished his pint and he agreed. Dejected, she began to gather a few of the gifts and cards and she read one, which said 'The Happy Couple.' She didn't know whether to laugh or cry, but felt too numb to do either. As she struggled to get through the door, trying to balance packages on top of her pregnant stomach, she cast a glance towards the bar and saw Cyril laughing, his face flushed with humour and alcohol. He was oblivious to her and she should have been angry, but she felt hurt. Only a couple of hours ago, he had apologised for his drunken behaviour and here he was, allowing his pregnant wife to struggle home with parcels meant as gifts to them both. She wished her father was here to guide her, but she knew it would be difficult to see him alone without raising her mother's suspicions. She couldn't let her mother know of her plight, she'd revel in it, shove her nose in it like an errant puppy.

She thought of Joan and how their friendship had rapidly deteriorated since Cyril had come on the scene. Had Joan seen something she hadn't? She had certainly shown no interest in Cyril, the wedding or the baby and had found a new friend to go out with. Dorothy thought back to the care-free evenings she'd enjoyed before that night at the dance. She remembered the times they would down sherries and port, then dance the night away. They would share their thoughts on everything; work, home and boys. It had always been a great outlet for Dorothy to meet up with Joan, to unburden her troubles and, more-often-than-not, to come away giggling. It seemed like a million miles away from what she had now. 'Be careful what you wish for,' she thought.

Dorothy struggled home and stumbled over the threshold. Once again, she was alone when she should have been with her husband. She placed the parcels on the armchair and slumped down on the settee, her lump serving as a reminder of just how trapped she really was. Without a child, her options may have been a little different but there was no escaping the responsibility of having another mouth to feed. Even if her mother had been a reasonable woman, the shame of going back home so soon after being married would be too much to bear. The whole street would point at her and know her as the poor little sod who couldn't even keep a husband for a month. That's how it was and nobody wanted to know about the whys and wherefores. They only saw the result, that you were no longer together and so you had failed. That was the trouble with falling pregnant so quickly, she hadn't had chance to discover the real character she was to marry. Her mother's words came back to haunt her, 'You've not known him two minutes, you don't know anything about him.' Although it pained Dorothy to admit it, her mother had been right.

Dorothy had never imagined, when she'd first cast eyes on that handsome young man at the door, the one who seemed so shy and charming, that it would result in this. When she first met him, she thought he was a polite and well-mannered young man. Now she knew him to be a thoughtless bigot who didn't care for anyone but himself. How could she have been so wrong? How had she misjudged him so? She concluded that the 'demon drink' had played a large part in the volatile nature of his character. His moods would swing from being loving, caring and thoughtful to being rude, abusive and sometimes aggressive. Her mother had always warned her about the 'demon drink' and how it could turn people. She'd never quite understood what she meant but 'my goodness,' she thought, 'I do now.'

Of course, there had been warnings of a selfish side to his nature. That day in the café when she told him she was pregnant and he seemed more concerned about finishing his egg and chips. He hadn't even put his arm around her when she'd cried, didn't seem to care at all. That time Dorothy had concluded that he had good reason to be upset after all that had happened with his mother. She'd forgiven him and it had blown over. They'd knuckled down to the tasks of finding a home and planning a wedding. They had discussed the baby and they were excited about the future. They had become much closer and Dorothy thought this was how it would be from then on, that they would become closer still and that they would build on their love for each other until nothing could tear them apart. How wrong she had been. Joan's words came to back to her and she winced at the truth of them, 'Mark my words,' she'd warned, 'as soon as he gets that ring on your finger, he'll change."

The first time he struck her, it hurt more inside than out. Dorothy had given up work in preparation for the imminent birth and money was tight. Cyril had taken to going for a pint most evenings after work with his friends from the shop, which didn't help matters at all. It wasn't every night, but it was enough to drain the finances, so that sometimes they'd go without a decent meal and have bread and butter instead. Pressure was bearing down on them both from all angles. When money was tight and food was sparse, Dorothy worried about her own health and that of her unborn child. What if it was born deformed because she didn't have the right food to eat? What if she didn't have the strength to cope with carrying the child, giving birth or feeding?

Cyril's moods had become increasingly unpredictable which meant that she never knew which face he would present when he arrived home. If he'd just had a couple, he could be the warmest, most affectionate husband she could wish for. A couple more and he'd be quiet and quite often morose, sinking into his own miserable world and not wanting to talk, not wanting her near him. The real concern for Dorothy though was when a couple of pints turned to seven. Lucky for some, but not in this household. She used to wonder how he could physically fit seven or eight pints in, but he seemed to do so with ease. Seven or eight pints and Cyril went from being reticent and deep, to openly abusive and aggressive. He'd come home wanting to pick an argument and it could be triggered by anything and everything. Dorothy found it impossible to avoid such conflicts. Try as she might to make sure everything was as good as it could be, there was always something he found lacking and it could be the smallest, most insignificant thing imaginable.

That's how it had been that first time. She had taken half an hour out from the household chores to put her feet up and eat. There was one last tin of beans in the cupboard and she decided to have them with some toast. As she buttered the toast, she salivated, she was so hungry. She ate like she'd never been fed, savouring every mouthful. When she'd finished, she'd made sure to clear away the dishes. She sat back in her arm chair and took another look around the living room which, as usual, was clean and tidy, 'like a new pin,' Dorothy thought.

Cyril arrived home at about eight thirty to find Dorothy snoozing in the chair. She opened one eye and struggled up, reading the expression on his face. This was not one of his happier moods. She went to greet him, not wanting him to think she was 'lazy' for staying in the chair. He stood, stock-still in front of her and looked at her with beery eyes, bloodshot with smoke and drink.

"What's for tea?" he snapped, as he walked over and opened the cupboard door.

Dorothy's stomach flipped as she realised it was almost devoid of food and she bit her lip as she waited for the inevitable. But what happened next took her completely by surprise. Just as she stepped forward to appease him with suggestions of what to eat, he spun around and struck her with such force that it knocked her backwards and she slumped, dazed, against the back wall of the kitchen. She put her hand up to her left cheek to stop the stinging, her eyes and mind trying to fathom just who this stranger was. Her cheekbone throbbed with hot pain and her pregnant stomach jarred awkwardly against her ribs, making it difficult to draw breath. She was too numb to cry and too shocked to move. Her husband seemed similarly afflicted. They locked eyes for a moment like a pair of alien species, each trying to make sense of the other, then slowly and painfully, Dorothy managed to stand and catch the breath which had eluded her for the past minute.

"I wanted those bloody beans!" he said and she looked in disbelief as he turned his back on her and rummaged through cupboards in search of food.

Dorothy sat at the kitchen table, head in hands and wept. Once again, her husband gave no indication at all that he cared in the least for the pain he had caused. She would have given anything to be back at home, going on nights out with Joan. Knowing what she knew now, she would have made a much better go at finding 'The One'. How could she have got 'Mr Right' so wrong?

She had got used to the verbal abuse, the odd little shove, but this was the first time he had hit her. Even through all the warning signs she hadn't seen it coming. She could see now though, that the increased intensity of his dark moods as the months went by was always going to lead to something bad, to this. A snippet of a conversation she had overheard on the factory floor between a woman, who had been similarly fated, and her wise friend came to mind. 'It'll only get worse from now on,' the wise one had said and the thought of this made Dorothy's spirits sink further. She sat there for a little while longer, then went wordlessly to bed, knowing anything she said would make matters worse. The frustration of not being able to find a solution to this problem, to Cyril, kept her awake. The more she thought about what had happened, the worse the palpitations became, until she thought her heart would give way any minute. Perhaps that would be best, she thought, at least then, I'd get some peace. With morbid thoughts of who would miss her if she died and what would happen to the baby, Dorothy eventually succumbed to slumber.

For the next few days Cyril was notably subdued, so much so that Dorothy thought an apology was imminent and she'd willed it to happen, but it didn't materialise. The disappointment lowered her mood even further and she went from being edgy and trying to please, to being sullen, dejected and apathetic. She no longer cared about the house being spotless and had even left dirty dishes in the sink from breakfast time, not having the energy to fret about what Cyril would say. Cyril said nothing, an indication to Dorothy that he must have felt something resembling remorse.

She was now very near to her due date and the physical and mental implications of the baby's arrival bore down on her and worried her sick. She knew this lull in Cyril's aggression wouldn't last forever and her thoughts were dominated by what would happen once the baby was born. An extra mouth to feed would mean further strain on the household finances and more pressure. More reason for Cyril to drink, increasing the likelihood of more violence. She had heard plenty of stories of girls who had violent husbands and she had thought them stupid for getting themselves into such a fix. Now here she was enduring the same predicament as those 'feckless wretches' she thought so weak for getting themselves trapped in the first place. She knew better now though, knew about the gradual slide into, and the impossible climb out of that pit. She knew how quickly you could go from being an independent working girl to being a helpless shadow of what you were, to being completely controlled by them so that you are nothing more than their chattel.

As if her life wasn't bad enough, just when she thought things couldn't get worse, she bumped into Joan, purely by chance as she stepped off the bus on the high street late one afternoon. Dorothy felt a fierce blush rising from her chest until it burned her whole face. She didn't know why she reacted in this way, only that she couldn't control it at all. Just as she pulled herself together enough to say 'hello,' Joan gave the smuggest sneer which quickly evolved into a short, mocking laugh. Dorothy was puzzled, it had been a while since they'd met up, but she couldn't fathom the meaning behind this greeting;

why the sniggering? Then Joan put her out of, or rather into, her misery.

"By heck you chose a right one there didn't you? Bet you wish we'd never stepped foot in that dancehall, don't you?"

"What do you mean?" asked Dorothy, dreading the response.

"Oh, come on, you must know, or if you don't, you're the only one in Eccles that doesn't."

"Know? Know what?" Dorothy whispered.

"That your husband's knocking about with some young tart from The Oddfellows. Bold as brass the pair of them, strutting down the streets like they've a right. Aye, and don't say you weren't warned. I knew he were trouble from the start and tried to tell you as much, more than once."

Dorothy stumbled back, reaching out for something to steady her. The pain she felt now was worse, by far, than the physical hurt she had felt when Cyril had struck her. She had a burning impulse to tear the child from within her and run for miles to where nobody was. She tried to move, but found herself rooted to the spot and unable to speak. Joan spun on her heel and headed off in the direction of home, stopping briefly to look back at Dorothy, with a softer look now, more of pity than disdain. This tipped Dorothy over the edge and she sobbed bitterly, her body wracked with misery. She paced the back streets aimlessly until the crying stopped and, limp with despair, she made her way back home. Once there, she crawled into bed without undressing, without eating, pulling the covers up tightly around her head which was about to explode with that damn song going round on a loop.

Dorothy woke when a new pain, physical this time, seared across her back and jolted her into consciousness. She rolled slowly onto her side and sat semi-upright, trying to breathe through what she now assumed to be the first contraction. The subsequent, unrelenting pains of labour relegated any thoughts of Cyril to a recess in her befuddled mind. Her body only had the strength to take on this new challenge, to get through this agony and produce her first-born. She managed one thought though; how fitting it was that Cyril wasn't here to support her, which made her wonder if there was anything right, anything good about this marriage. She managed to get herself up and she stumbled awkwardly and slowly down the stairs. She rested at the bottom, then slid her shoes on and shuffled next door.

"Hey up Dorothy, whatever's the matter?" was the greeting, as Mrs Barker opened the front door to see her neighbour almost crouching in agony on her step.

"It's coming, the baby," Dorothy whispered as she grabbed the door jamb for support.

"Oh, oh, of course, the baby, of course it is. Now you come in and I'll send for Mrs Brown. Don't you worry about a thing, it'll be over in no time love. Where's your Cyril?"

"*My* Cyril is at work, or at least I think he is, although he could be anywhere, with anyone, who knows?"

"Eee, you're not making much sense love; come in now and we'll get you comfortable. Frank, Frank! Be a love and get Mrs Brown to come. Quick sharp now Frank, hurry up."

Frank appeared in the doorway from the kitchen, clutching his newspaper and looking somewhat bewildered and bedraggled as if he'd been roused from a deep sleep. When he saw Dorothy, so fully pregnant and in pain, he leaped into action as if he'd sat inadvertently in the embers of the fire, which were glowing comfortingly in the grate. Despite the warmth in the room, Dorothy wanted to be home, wanted to be in her own bed and stay there for as long as she possibly could.

"Would you mind helping me back home, only I'd rather be there, you know."

"Course, course I will love," and with that, Mrs Barker, a woman of slight proportions, hooked Dorothy's arm around her shoulder and took her weight as well as she could. She beckoned for her husband to do the same and, together, they shuffled next door so that Dorothy could have her wish.

It was a struggle to get Dorothy upstairs but they eventually managed and she was settled into bed and made as comfortable as she could be. Within the hour, Mrs Brown, the local Midwife, arrived on her bicycle, equipped with the leather bag containing all the things she would need to assist the birth. For Dorothy, there was less breathing space now between pains, which were increasingly intense and almost unbearably long. She had never been so glad to see the reassuringly stout figure of the woman who had guided her through this pregnancy. As the midwife strode across the bedroom with an air of ownership, Dorothy knew she was in safe hands and she smiled weakly as, Mrs Barker on the one side held her hand and Mrs Brown, on the other, busied herself with preparations. Frank made his excuses and left Dorothy in capable hands.

Cyril arrived home some time later to find the front door ajar and a bicycle propped up against the wall. He immediately recognised it as that belonging to the lady he'd often seen cycling determinedly through neighbouring streets, 'the baby lady.' All previous thoughts and actions seemingly erased from his mind, he pushed open the door and flew upstairs to the source of the gentle voices of women intent on seeing a task through.

When he crouched beside her, Dorothy wanted desperately to hurt him, but only had the strength to look sideways at him, hoping he could read the despair in her eyes. Wanting to punish him, but wanting more for him to hold her through this agony, she reached out for his hand, and taking this as permission, he held hers so tightly it hurt with bittersweet pain. They locked eyes for a moment, Dorothy searching for goodness in the pools of brown that swam before her. She was sure she saw a glimmer of something; love, regret, remorse; she wasn't sure, but for the first time in what seemed like ages, they worked as a team. Cyril held her hands as she pushed with all she was worth, the midwife offering words of encouragement and advice. At the end of their efforts the child was born and Dorothy leaned forward.

"A bouncing baby boy," replied Mrs Brown, "what will you call him?"

They hadn't had the inclination to sit down and talk baby names in the days preceding this one.

"Frank," said Dorothy, for it seemed only fair and

fitting that she named him after the man next door who had shown compassion and care in her hour of need.

The midwife held him up by the feet until he let out his first cry. He was bloody and slimy and beautiful. Dorothy forgot the pain and held out her arms so that she could receive her son. As she cradled him, Cyril looked on. Dorothy didn't know if the look on his face was wonder or fear, but she didn't care. Little Frank seemed perfect in every way, from the shock of black hair to his tiny waxy feet and Dorothy wondered how something so beautiful could have been born from such dire circumstances.

She was relieved that her baby appeared not to have been affected by the negative physical and mental pressures which had impacted so strongly on her life leading up to this moment. She wondered how she could ever have thought about ridding herself of this little bundle of sweet charm, shuddered at the thought of wanting to rip this baby physically from her being. 'I must have been in a right state,' she reasoned 'and we all know who was to thank for that.' But if anyone had walked in on that scene, they would have thought Cyril the epitome of a proud new dad, a family man. For he held the baby so tenderly in his strong arms, he looked like the vision of a great protector.

For a few days, Dorothy's priority was to establish herself as a new mum, to be good at it, to do a better job than her own mother had. She knew, as she nursed her son, that she had never experienced love before, because this love had a whole new dimension to it. This child had taken over her whole being and had given her life a new meaning and purpose. The joy she felt when those bleary little eyes tried to focus on her face was like no other joy on Earth. For a while at least, her life took a turn for the better and she concentrated her energies on tending to her new-born.

Cyril was like a different person, possibly because his trips to the pub, apart from 'wetting the baby's head' had now reduced significantly. Dorothy relaxed into this new way of being, but knew the bubble had to burst sooner or later, not because she was a pessimist, but because she was a realist. About a month after the birth, galvanised by Cyril's displays of affection, she found the courage to confront him. She hadn't forgotten her encounter with Joan and the news she shared, or was it gossip? Dorothy needed to know, she couldn't be made a fool of for the rest of her life, she was worth more than that.

"Right, I'm not going to beat about the bush," she said one night after supper, when she sensed Cyril was restless and fidgety, as if he wanted to be somewhere else.

"You've been spotted, stepping out with some young girl, making a fool of me, as if I wasn't fool enough for marrying you in the first place."

"What?" Cyril asked, as he turned around to face his wife, to face the inevitable showdown, the big truth, the payback for all his reckless, thoughtless actions.

"What do you mean, I've been spotted? Who's told you that?"

"Never mind who's told me that. Is it true?"

"It was that interfering cow, Joan, wasn't it? Best thing you ever did was to break ties with her. She comes back on the scene and there's trouble straight away."

Dorothy stood resolute and faced her husband square-on. "I just want the truth Cyril," she said wearily, "are you seeing another woman behind me back because if you are, be man enough to admit it."

"Man enough? I'll tell you what I'm man enough to do, walk away from a stupid row caused by gossip between two women who have nothing better to do. I don't have to stand here and listen to this."

That Brylcreemed quiff that she used to love so much hung down now and covered half of Cyril's reddened face. That wave of thick dark hair was no longer something which endeared her to him. He flicked it sharply to one side in the heat of his anger. It now served to irritate her, to emphasise his quick hot temper and she was beginning to despise it. She thought how pathetic he looked as he strode away from her, his trousers hanging from his thin backside. He seemed to have shrunk, the result perhaps of erratic eating habits due to his drinking. Or did he just appear to be smaller as her respect for him waned? He slipped on his jacket and without a word, he went out, slamming the door with such force that the window shook in its frame.

"Good riddance," whispered Dorothy, then she slumped into her armchair, her place of solace and she looked at her son and wondered what would come next for them.

Once the seed of irritation with Cyril had been planted in Dorothy's mind it seemed to take on a life of its own, to grow exponentially until it took control of her and governed her every thought and move. That back of his which was once a haven of comfort when she snuggled into it, now only served as a solid reminder of Cyril's inability to commit. She watched it so often as he walked away from one situation or another; it had come to represent a door repeatedly closing on them and shutting her out of his life. Once so broad and protective, it now seemed narrow, weak and bony. With his ribs clearly visible and his shoulder blades protruding sharply at the top, this back now represented a lack of substance. That beautiful quiff which used to make her insides tingle had become nothing more than an irritation. The way it flopped over one eye when he was angry made her want to rip it from its roots, and he was angry so often these days. Dorothy wondered how the very attributes which had attracted her so much to Cyril had so quickly become the source of resentment.

Being at home with the baby had given Dorothy time to reflect on her own life with her parents, to analyse their relationship in the light of her own. Did they once love each other, before it deteriorated into tolerance? Could her mother have been affectionate and loving once upon a time before the man of her dreams became an annoyance? Was it the toils of life, of marriage, that turned her miserable or was she always that way? Somewhere along the way, Dorothy was sure that her mother had stood in the way of Medusa's stare and had been turned completely to stone, unable to feel anything for anyone. Dorothy feared that the same would happen to her if she continued in this loveless marriage. Her biggest fear was that these resentments would slowly eat away at her until she was nothing. Surely, eventually, you would have to preserve your sanity by shutting yourself off from those who hurt you. By ossifying your soul, you could save your mind. The thought of becoming so stony cold that you couldn't offer your children any love was the most frightening thing that could happen to any mother. But Dorothy feared that the process had already begun. She had become so increasingly irritated by Cyril's ways that she felt there was no way back, not that she wanted to go back, to a time before her beloved son. Her son was the only one who could soothe her and her husband was the one person who could make her heckles rise so swiftly she didn't have time to think about how the resultant outburst would affect the boy.

When Frank was born, Dorothy had been overwhelmed by an enormous surge of love for him. She thought she would never let him out of her sight for fear he would somehow perish without her. That love was now overshadowed with guilt for all the anger and hatred he had to endure just by being born into this mess. She realised that her attempts at parenting were no better than her mother's and the thought of that disturbed her to the core. She had meant to do so much better, she was going to give her children everything she hadn't had; love, security, affection and a calm and stable home. How had it come to this? She liked to think that it wasn't her fault, that if Cyril had been different, everything would be better. That thought assuaged the guilt, but only temporarily. Dorothy was clever and capable of deep thought. She knew in her heart that she was partly to blame for choosing Cyril as her husband. She should have heeded the warning signs; his reluctance to comfort her when she was most in need, his inability to commit fully to the family they had made. His desire to cavort with other women. Why had she been so blind to his faults? Had she been so desperate to settle, to escape her own home, that she just didn't see that she was going from one hell to another? Or was it his indefatigable charm that had won her over and kept her entranced? She didn't have any answers, she only knew that she was desperately unhappy and the harder she tried to come up with a solution, the more she realised that there wasn't one. At least not an easy one anyway. What were the options? To go back to her mother's house and spend the rest of her life being labelled as the girl with the bastard child. To go back to work and leave Frank with her mother. To go through life with the stigma of being a divorcee. How would she find a decent husband then, someone who would take on Frank? The only other option would be to stay in the house and get Cyril to leave, then pay her enough maintenance to survive on. This made Dorothy laugh, it was so unlikely.

There was no doubt about it, she was trapped in this life, there was no feasible alternative. She would just have to 'grin and bear it,' as she had to 'grin and bear' so many things before.

CHAPTER 5

The Accident
1955

There was a stout shadow at the front door and, for once, it wasn't Cyril. She knew this to be so. It stood stock still for a start and surely, after five hours on the ale, he'd be rocking by now. Why was she instilled with the same sense of dread then, as if it *was* him? She unlatched the door and slowly pulled it inwards. It was then that the dread really took hold. The uniform hit her senses with the same wallop as his fists. She feared that something had happened to Frank.

"Mrs Benson?"

"Yes."

"Is Cyril Benson your husband?"

"Yes, he is."

"I'm afraid I've some really bad news."

'Let him be dead,' she thought.

"He's been involved in a bad accident. He's in Hope Hospital. If you want to get a few things together, we can take you there now."

"Right, well I'll have to ask the neighbour to look after the kids. Come in, I won't be long."

Dorothy took off her apron and tried to wear a look

of concern. She busied herself putting away baking equipment, secretly planning her life without him.

"I'm afraid, you'll have to leave that Mrs Benson, we need to go pretty soon."

"Why, is he that bad?"

"We don't really know how bad he is yet, we just need to get you there."

"Oh."

She tried to hide her disappointment. So, he wasn't on his death bed after all. She grabbed her cardigan and the youngest and walked around to her neighbour's house. She knocked on the back door, peering through the window as she did so. Margaret opened the door and asked her what was wrong.

"It's Cyril, he's had an accident," she said.

Although she had often confided in Margaret, she didn't want her to think she was heartless by adding, 'pity it wasn't worse.'

"Can you mind little 'un by any chance and get the others from school at half past? I don't know how long I'll be."

"Course I can love, give him here. I'll pick them up and I'll give them some tea, so don't worry. I'll see you when you get back. I hope he's alright love."

Dorothy smiled weakly, pushing down the 'I don't' that threatened to escape.

In the car on the way to hospital, the officer explained that Cyril and his friend had been drinking. They'd apparently intended to leave the car there, but, after a few, had decided to drive somewhere else. The car was found turned over on an embankment. Cyril was trapped and had to be cut free, but they had both survived. Cyril had broken both legs and was in Hope Hospital, the irony of the name not lost on Dorothy. Her face dropped as she thought about her plight; three kids, a crippled husband and a rented house which was in his name. If Dorothy looked miserable on the journey to see her husband, it wasn't because she was worried about him, but because her chances of escape had just narrowed to almost zero in one careless and thoughtless act.

When she finally arrived at the ward, Dorothy was shown to Cyril's bed. She only knew it was him by that damned quiff which was flopping out of the bandages around his head. His face was purple, not with anger, but with bruising. He was comatose and helpless. One leg was suspended in the air on traction, the spindly form of the other outlined beneath the counterpane. What would other wives do? Weep and howl and wish him better? She felt nothing. Now that the others had gone, she couldn't even bring herself to hold his hand, couldn't be bothered to keep up the pretence. All she could think was 'you selfish bastard.' She sat down beside the bed and stared at the mess before her, the mess that she had once idolised, then feared. His mouth hung open, dry spittle and blood congealed in each corner. His thin arms flopped limply at his sides and his chest sunk like a failed sponge cake. How had this man exerted such power over her?

After an unsuccessful operation to repair his broken bones and subsequent episodes of infection, Cyril was released from hospital. He was by no means healed as the infections had left him with open ulcers which needed to be cleaned and dressed daily. Due to the breaks, he walked with a distinctive limp. However, he still managed to hobble to the pub most evenings. Dorothy's situation became even worse than it was before the accident, his moods even darker and less predictable. He was in constant pain and he and was frustrated by his impaired mobility. He lashed out in anger at whoever was nearest, whether that was Dorothy or one of the kids.

"Pass me that dressing case, will you?"

"Which one dad?"

"What do you mean, which one? Are you taking the piss? The one I use every bleeding day, that's which one!"

The leg was exposed in all its green and gory glory. Frank walked past his father and was felled by a blow to the head, uncalled for and unexpected. He crouched down, holding his head in his hands, unable to move with the effort of trying to stem the tears.

"Get up, you soft shite or I'll give you something to cry about! Tell your mother to pass me the dressing case, NOW!"

The boy half-stood and scuttled off to the kitchen, still nursing his head.

"My dad wants his dressing case mam," he stuttered, between sobs.

"What's up, has he hit you? I've told you to keep away from him when he's in this mood. Go and get his case, it's by the chair. Hurry up, quick as you can. Quick sharp Frank!"

"Can you get it mam? He might hit me again."

"Don't be daft, go and get it, be sharp."

Frank reluctantly sloped back into the living room, trying to avoid eye contact with his father. He walked around the back of the settee, reached for the case and quickly handed it over. His father's face was red again, so the boy backed up towards the door, slipped out and went upstairs.

"Dorothy! Come and help me with this will you?"

Dorothy tensed, "I'm doing the tea, I can't be everywhere."

Cyril flashed up again, "Is there anyone in this fucking house who has a clue what to do? You're bleeding hopeless, the lot of you!"

Since she saw him so helpless in his hospital bed, Dorothy had become less fearful of her husband and more intolerant. She had become almost immune to his outbursts, but she knew if she left him any longer he would deteriorate into a raging ogre and the kids would suffer. She put down the potato and the peeler and went to him, trying to defuse the situation by dressing the wound calmly, quietly, all the while simmering underneath, her stomach clenched and the bile rolling around inside. If this was her lot in life, she'd rather be dead.

His days were spent drinking in his favourite haunt, where he 'held court' to a few of his cronies. He returned in the evening for another session and rolled home somewhere around midnight, only to start the routine again the next day. It started with a bang on the floor for his morning cup of tea, then he would get up, get dressed, have breakfast and he would be out by eleven. He would return around four, eat, get ready and go out again. Dorothy knew that he earned some money doing 'deals' in the pub, but she knew better than to probe.

Him having control of the money, meant that Dorothy was completely at his mercy, and she had to tread very carefully or else the children may not get enough to eat. This was bad enough but, when he wanted sex, he would force himself upon her and she had no choice but to comply. With the threat of withholding the money, he had her over the proverbial barrel. There was one saving grace, after what happened to his own mother, he didn't hit her when she was pregnant, fearful of where it would lead. That would explain why Dorothy was pregnant again, with her fourth child, even though they could ill afford it and it was the last thing Dorothy needed. The midwife had advised her not to have any more, that her body was weak and malnourished, having endured three, now four pregnancies in quick succession. When it came to contraception, Cyril was not taking on that responsibility, his complete disregard for the well-being of his family meant that it was all on Dorothy's shoulders. When she suggested sterilization, he threw the idea out straight away, citing his Catholic religion. That was a joke, he hadn't stepped foot in a church in all the time she'd known him. It was Dorothy who had to deal with the pregnancies, with the extra mouths to feed and, what's more, there had been no talk of stopping at four. She wondered how many children she would have to bear before her body completely gave up. The doctor had told her that a woman's body could still bear children up to being in her fifties. At this rate, that could mean another ten! Dorothy could only hope that she became infertile before then, or fate intervened in a different way. It was difficult to see a way out of this 'life' and she was becoming increasingly frustrated at the injustice.

She was nothing but a slave who was imprisoned by her own husband.

Dorothy finished the dressing, then returned to the kitchen to tend to Frank who had crept back down stairs.

"What's for tea mam?" one of the others called.

"Shit with sugar on," she called back, as she wiped away Frank's tears.

That made Frank smile and she smiled too. Moments like this were rare and they had to cherish them.

CHAPTER 6

The Birth
1961

Dorothy held the child in her arms. It was her seventh, her fourth daughter. She could hear the voices of children outside and she realised it must be the end of school. The midwife finished washing her hands and walked over to Dorothy's bed.

"That was a tough delivery Dorothy, not only because the baby was big, but because you've had so many, love. I know it's not what you want to hear, but the doctor was right, you need to stop at this one. They advised you after three not to have any more, your body's not up to it love, as young as you are."

Dorothy's expression didn't give much away. She was tired, not just tired but fatigued and her body throbbed with pain.

"I know what you're saying Ann, but you try and push a sixteen-stone man off you when he wants his way. You try and explain the basics of contraception when he's had nine pints. You try and tell him that another child might be the difference between eating and not."

She wept then, became inconsolable. The midwife took the baby and placed her in the makeshift cot, a drawer at the bottom of the chest in the bedroom.

"I'm sorry love. I wasn't trying to make you feel bad, I just care about your health. Has Cyril thought about having the snip? Sorry to be so blunt."

"I wish he would, and I wish they'd use a blunt knife an' all," came Dorothy's reply.

The midwife laughed then and they chatted about how Dorothy would cope with seven children, how she'd feed them, clothe them and get them to school on time. They talked about how the elder three, the boys, didn't know a nappy from a hankie and how the girls, at six, four and two, were too young to be of any real help. It was all down to Dorothy. Not only did she have to cope with seven children, but with the biggest and most selfish child of them all, Cyril. She could have done a better job, she was sure, without him there, but she was stuck with him. Even though he was always complaining about how useless she was, he didn't show any signs of leaving. Why would he when he was free to come and go as he pleased in a home where he was in control?

The midwife cleaned up and had one last peep at the sleeping baby.

"What are you going to call her? Have you got a name?"

"Alison, after a lady who used to live on our street when I was a kid. She used to give me bread and butter when me mam wouldn't let me in. I think she felt sorry for me. She'd turn in her grave if she could see me now, what I've become."

"Come on love, it's not that bad. You've got seven healthy kids, good neighbours and you can always talk to me, you know that."

Dorothy smiled and nodded, "I know, but it's hard Ann and I'm tired."

"Of course, I know you are love, but you're a trooper and you'll get through, like you always have."

Ann promised Dorothy that she'd call tomorrow and then left, just as Cyril arrived home, swaying slightly and filling the doorway with the sheer size of him.

'God help her,' thought the midwife. "You've got another girl," she called back to Cyril, then she rode off, unwilling to hear the drivel that would emanate from his drunken mouth.

Cyril staggered in, hardly registering that there was another addition to his growing brood. He was more concerned about finding food than he was about Dorothy or the baby.

"It's a girl, dad," said Sylvia, the eldest girl.

"Another one?" he replied, then carried on with his search.

Sylvia scuttled back upstairs and sat around her mother's bed with the others, fussing over the new baby.

"Where's your father?" asked Dorothy.

"He's in the kitchen looking for food," said Sylvia.

"He'll be lucky," she replied, then flopped back on to the pillow and closed her weary eyes.

It had always been difficult for Dorothy to provide food for the children and each birth had put her under more pressure. Another child did not necessarily mean an increase in the money which Cyril handed over each week, that depended largely on his mood and how well she could appease him. Having more children had only made the situation worse and she was tired. Her only release was her regular chats with Margaret, the neighbour, who treated her to cream cakes and lent a listening ear. Cyril didn't like it, but it was that or 'put my head in the gas oven,' Dorothy had told him. She needed the chats to stop her from going mad. She had often worried about her mental health, wondered why she felt so little for the children she had borne, but she concluded that anyone would struggle to love so many kids, especially with a husband like Cyril adding to the pressure.

The cot had to be slotted into the corner of the front bedroom, in the gap between the two beds where the other girls slept. Dorothy could only hope that this would be the last time she would have to fit another baby into this tiny house.

Trying to make sleeping arrangements for seven kids and two adults was difficult enough, but it wasn't the biggest challenge for Dorothy. She had to find the strength to provide meals, clean the house, clothe the kids, get them to school, appease Cyril and avoid getting pregnant again. The last two were mutually bound; how could she do one without the other?

Life went on in the Benson household, the children growing, the arguments becoming more frequent and more violent. The pattern of life had set into a daily routine, which went something like this; the elder kids got up first, then woke up and dressed the younger ones. Dorothy would come down some time during this chaos and finish off what her children had started. Inevitably there would be the bang on the bedroom floor, Cyril, letting it be known he was ready for his morning cup of tea. One of the kids would take him his tea, walking up the stairs carefully, always knocking on the door and delivering the cup to the bedside table without comment and avoiding eye contact. The kids would go to school, Dorothy would start the chores, Cyril would get up and get ready for his first session at the pub, then he'd leave. The kids would come home from school, Cyril would come home from the pub, tea would be made and eaten, homework done amidst the mayhem and noise of siblings fighting and Cyril shouting at one or other of them, or at Dorothy, then he would go back out for the evening session. At the end of the evening, there was a massive metaphorical holding of breath whilst the whole household awaited his return, speculating about his mood. The younger ones would cling to their blankets as his key went in the door and heavy footfalls followed. They waited for clues as to what state he was in. Sometimes he would stagger, laughing as he stumbled, sometimes he would shout at whoever was brave enough to be up and pick an aggressive argument, mostly with Dorothy.

"Look at the state of you, you're nothing but a whore! Yeah, go on, cry, you'll piss less."

"Where are those daughters of yours? Out whoring? Just like their mother, useless piece of shite, you're nothing else!"

Then the banging, the pleading, the crying, the hitting, until one of the lads came to the rescue.

"Leave her alone, you drunken bastard. Come on mam, come to bed now, leave him here."

"Ah, you skinny-arsed soft shite. Women are only after

one thing and that's the money in your pocket. Believe me, they need a crack to keep 'em in order."

The older children were becoming more aware and more affected by the rows. The boys tried to protect their mother, but they were cautious; one swipe could send them across the room. The girls tried to do as they were told mostly and to stay out of his way. The little ones were demanding and seemed to be cursed by an endless hunger, much to the despair of Dorothy who barely managed to eke the food out to the end of the week. Clothes and shoes were passed down to the next child and Dorothy made use of her sewing skills to make simple dresses. Generally, the children were good at school, but occasionally, Dorothy would be called in to deal with one misdemeanour or another; the boys fighting, the girls caught stealing from the snack box, nothing major, but enough to send Dorothy over the edge sometimes and she would lash out and give them a good smack around the head or the backs of their legs. Neighbours rallied round with knits for the babies and cast-offs for the others, but they never really knew the true extent of Dorothy's misery.

Despite all the problems, the family was still able to use humour as a way of getting through the hard times. There was light-hearted teasing and taunting, each child having their own nick-name. There were the silly tricks they played on each other and the impersonations they performed with such accuracy. Teachers, actors and family members were mimicked to perfection and the laughter would ring through the house. But only when he wasn't there.

There were some occasions when the neighbours got

together and celebrated, such as Bonfire Night when there would always be a huge fire at the corner house. Potatoes would be put at the bottom of it and Guy Fawkes at the top and the children would run around with their sparklers, squealing with delight. The mothers would gather round, gazing into the flames while they gossiped and shared problems. Fathers would light fireworks, throw more wood on the fire; doors, crates, pallets and anything else they could get their hands on, then they'd slope off the pub and leave the women to it.

Birthdays were a problem for Dorothy as she never had money to indulge her children with a gift and Cyril never remembered them. She knew the children felt it because they asked questions like 'how come we don't get presents mam or have parties like other people do?' One of them even invited school friends round on her Birthday once, just so she could feel 'normal', like them. She hid behind the dustbins when the first one arrived with a present, all tied up with a big silk bow. She saw the confusion on her mother's face, the disappointment on her friend's face as she walked away and she cried for the present she would never have and the embarrassment of school on Monday.

Life was tough but it went on. Meals were made, clothes were washed, bottoms changed, knees grazed and cleaned up, legs slapped, floors scrubbed, homework done, games played and babies quieted. All in the chaos of a household of nine in a house with three bedrooms.

CHAPTER 7

Snippets of the childhood of Alison Benson
1965 – 1980

It's my first day at school and I'm sitting by the bookshelf trying to make myself smaller. That's what I do when the noise gets too much. My mum calls me a 'little mouse', says she never knows I'm there, I'm that quiet. That's why I do it so they don't know I'm there, so they'll leave me alone, like I want to be left alone now. I don't understand why everyone else looks so happy and smiley when all I want to do is to roll up in a ball. The teacher has a kind face and she kneels next to me trying to make me come out. She smells nice, like Sunday bath time. She wears a pale blue jumper which is clean and neat with a lovely necklace hanging down. I take hold of her hand and she pulls me up then takes me to a table where some others are playing with Lego. She tells them to play nicely, then she walks away and leaves me there. I don't feel comfortable sitting here, I want to crawl back to my corner, like I do at home. The others are all playing and smiling, passing the Lego around and building little houses. They don't want to play with me, so I just sit and watch quietly, hoping they don't notice me. When it's story time, we're told to tidy up. I sit, engrossed, as the teacher with the kind face, tells the tale of Hansel and Gretel. I feel a funny ache inside as she tells us about the little boy and the girl who don't have enough to eat, about the step mother who doesn't like them. Everyone gasps when the wife tells her husband to leave the children in the forest, but I don't. I wish I could go to the forest with them. After school, I look for my mam in the crowd. Children run towards their mothers, holding out pictures they have painted. They look so excited and their mams look pleased to see them. I watch them as they take the pictures and plant kisses on the sides of faces, flatten down stray hairs with their fingers which they've spat on. My mam stands there looking into space, no smile. When I walk towards her, she doesn't register until I wave my hands in front of her. Then she looks at me through dull eyes, takes the break off the pram and moves off. I grab hold of the handle and skip to keep up. She doesn't look at me, just stares ahead. She doesn't ask about my day, so I don't tell her. I don't tell her about the kind teacher and Hansel and Gretel.

We're in the hall, waiting for assembly to start. My jumper is making me itch because it's too tight and scratchy. I've just noticed the dirt on my knees, so I try to cover it up with my skirt, but it won't reach. The boy next to me tuts, so I try to sit still and I make myself as small as I can by putting my knees together, so I don't touch him. I can sense him looking at me, so I stare towards the front, trying to keep my face and body still. I feel that sting you get when you need a wee, but I'm too scared to ask, so I jiggle my bottom on the hall floor, hoping I can last until the end, but I don't think I can. Then, I'm desperate to go, but I can't get up now because assembly is about to start and everyone will look at me. I can't hold the wee in any longer, so I have to let it go. I feel the warm trickle and hope it doesn't make a big puddle, hope my clothes soak it up so the boy next to me can't see what I've done. All through assembly, I worry that the kids behind can see the wet patch and I'm waiting for one of them to poke me in the back, but they don't. At the end, we start to walk out in a line and I quickly step away from my place, from the dark patch on the wooden floor, but one of the teachers notices it. She checks our bottoms one-by-one. I start to shake and cry and she pulls me out. I'm so ashamed of what I've done, but she doesn't hit me. She takes hold of my hand and takes me to the back of the classroom where there's a box full of spare clothes. She finds me some clean knickers and shorts to put on, then she takes me to the toilets and I get changed, wondering what she thinks of me. When I look up at her, she is smiling at me and I don't understand why she isn't annoyed. 'I'm sorry miss,' I say. She takes my hand and takes me back to class. Everyone looks at me and some of them snigger, but the teacher carries on with her lesson and, eventually, they all look back at her. I sit at the back of the classroom looking at my skinny knees full of dirt, sticking out from another person's shorts. I cross my legs so they're less visible. The teacher beckons me to sit with the others and they snigger as I walk towards them in too-short shorts and baggy knickers. I kneel on the floor, curling my legs underneath. The teacher talks louder and they all turn to face her and pretend they're listening, but I can see the nudges, the heads together, forehead against forehead, the shoulders shaking with mirth, the sly looks. I unhook my legs and fold my knees to my chest, burying my head so they might not see me.

If they can't see me, I'm not here. When I get home, I walk in with my head down waiting for my mam to ask about the shorts, but she's not there. I get changed and come down stairs. I look for her through all the rooms. The baby's in his wooden high chair, banging on the tray and looking at me. I look in all the cupboards but can only find some flour, a bag of sugar and a tin of tomatoes. There's nothing I could give to the baby, so I play 'peek-a-boo' with him. It's nearly dark and I wonder where my mam is, but I don't want to leave the baby, so I lift him out. I walk through the house again, but she's nowhere. The older ones come home from school and ask what I'm doing on my own in the house with the baby. I tell them she isn't here, that I've looked everywhere but she isn't here. They look at each other in a worried way, then we hear the latch on the back door being lifted. The neighbour comes in with my mam, her face is red and puffy and she looks sad, like someone's died. She tries to go back out of the house again but the neighbour talks to her and tells her to stay. She plonks herself down on the chair, not looking at us or talking to us, then she goes upstairs and we don't see her for the rest of the night.

I'm at the teacher's desk. It's my turn to read. The teacher asks me to read from the beginning and when I do, she looks surprised. She tells me I'm a good reader and my heart swells in my chest. She gives me the next book in the range, the more difficult one and she tells me to take it home and practise. I'm so proud of my book, I hide it under the bed and take it out every evening to read over and over. I like reading the books my teacher gives me, but my brothers and sisters tease me. 'You'll turn into a book,' they say, but I don't care. When they snatch it from me and start throwing it around, then I care, because books are precious, that's what miss says. I don't know why it's only me who likes to read in our house. One day, I'm behind the settee reading when I hear the front door go. My body stiffens, as it always does. My dad comes in and in one swift move, he knocks the book out of my hand and hits me across the face. It stings like mad and I get up and run upstairs out of the way. I hear them shouting. The noise rings through the house, then I hear a door slam and my mam clatters up the stairs. I go to see if she's alright, but she knocks me away and I fall into the washing basket. I get up to go back in my room, but there are splodges of blood along the floorboards of the landing, so I go to the bathroom to get a cloth. My mam is leaning over the bath, her nose dripping blood onto the white enamel. I ask her if she's alright and she tell me to 'sod off.' She's crying and I don't know what to do, but I've already been hit and knocked into the washing basket, so I go and wash the blood up.

The beast is on his throne, his face grey, not puce, not filled with violent rage but just simmering with quiet contempt and disgust. I can hear my mother's pathetic sobs and pleas. She has been locked out into the bitter cold winter night. She's knocking on the window, but we can't see her because the curtains are drawn. We can only hear the sobs and the knocks, hear her begging us to let her in. When I emptied the bin earlier, before she was thrown out, there was a layer of furry frost on the top of the black lid. I made clouds with my breath in the air and almost slipped on the ice around the grid as I ran in out of the cold. It's freezing out there and I'm desperate to let her in, knowing that her nightie is probably turning stiff, like the washing does when you leave it out too late on a night like this. Along with the others, I plead with my father to let her in, but 'no,' the beast says, 'let her stay where she belongs, on the street. She can freeze out there, for all I care. She can cry all night, she's not coming in.' He tells us how useless she is, how he has to get his own tea these days because she's always out and when she isn't she 'sits there snivelling, saying nothing.' He tells us that she doesn't deserve to come back in until she can sort herself out, make herself useful. My mother is an outcast, cast out, no longer required, unwanted and of no value. Just like me, I think and I wonder when it will be my turn to be thrown out.

The sound of the key turning in the lock jolts me from my slumber. Curled up, as ever, in the foetal position, I stiffen and listen, clinging on to my knees. The unmistakable lopsided thudding of heavy feet along the Lino of the corridor announces his return. Lopsided because of his accident which left one leg shorter than the other. His short leg doesn't bend either, so he swings it outwards when he needs to sit down. He always moans that he can't go to the picture house because of his leg, but he never went anyway. Why are we so scared of a man who can't even run? Because his voice is like thunder and he can knock you across the room with one swipe. The return of the beast, the lopsided beast, to his lair and the stuff he hates most, women and kids, 'nothing worse.' I listen and wait, wondering what mood he's in. Will he be in a rage? Will it be an aggressive rant about something that doesn't matter, like a dirty tea cup on the side? Crime of crimes. Or will it be the beast as a generous child-man, doling out Mars Bars to the kids he occasionally remembers to acknowledge? Will it just be the 'indifferent' entrance and subsequent falling into bed without bothering anyone? I never know, but it's the waiting that makes my heart beat fast, makes me scared. It's these glimpses though, of the beast as human, displaying 'normal' behaviour, such as giving and laughing, that torture me, make me think that things could be different. Because I am beginning to feel that things should be different and I can't understand why the beast that is my father didn't choose another way of life. Things could be so much better if he just let us be and stopped raging at us, stopped hitting my mam and being cruel, she doesn't do him any harm. I don't understand. I know my mam doesn't say much or do much these days, but that doesn't mean he has to keep hitting her. I wish she could be like other mothers. The ones I have seen at school are happy and smart. They wear brown shoes and nylons, pretty blouses and make up. My mam always has that apron on with the smears of cake mix all over it. She always has flour in her hair and a sad look on her face. Sometimes she has bruises and black eyes and she never smiles or talks. I wish she was like the others, but she isn't. I wonder why. Does my dad hit her because she doesn't smile any more, or does she not smile because my dad hits her? She used to smile. The others used to laugh at her and laugh with her and there'd be fun in the house, but now there's only crying and hitting and shouting and she sits in a corner or disappears or goes to bed.

There's an ugly scene unfolding in the living room. The beast has a face like an over-ripe plum and eyes as black as flint marbles. His mouth is twisted and emanates angry words, as twisted in their accusations as the mouth from which they spew. Words aimed at my mother; 'whore,' 'lazy slut,' 'money-grabbing cow.' His black quiff, normally perfectly groomed hangs down now and he flicks it back out of his face with a jerk of his head to reveal the angry twist of his mouth and that Kirk Douglas cleft in his chin. Then a silver flash, and the knife is up at my mother's throat. He backs her against the wall and she stands with her arms out at each side of her, unable to push him away because there isn't a gap between their bodies. Her eyes are bulging with terror and I think she's going to die. My legs give way and I crumple on the floor, but I don't think anybody notices because they're all frozen. Then someone lifts me up and carries me off upstairs. It's my brother. "Come on, come into bed with me." What happens next is horrible, shameful and I screw my eyes up tight and scream a silent scream inside. A song starts to go around in my head, one that has been on the radio. 'This could be the last time, this could be the last time, maybe the last time, I don't know-ow, der der der dum.' Around and around on repeat in my head, 'this could be the last time, this could be the last time, maybe the last time, I don't know-ow,' again and again, an unending loop of words I've picked up from the radio. Then his weight is no longer on me, but the song stays. I lie there like a dead person, dead in and out, except for the song which won't leave me. Nothing and nobody makes sense. He unlocks the door and goes back to his pretending. Pretending to be a caring soul who rescues people while all the while he breaks them, bit by bit. I know the truth.

I don't know how it happened or why but the beast has left. He still comes around, though, shouting the odds, banging with his massive fists on the back door. He tells her, and anyone else who's listening that it's 'his' house, tells her to get out of his house, the rent book is in his name. Performing like a tethered, dancing bear, whilst we tremble in a corner like bait. Striking out, just as threatening as any wild beast with claws and teeth. Inside, we shake in fear that he'll breach the defence. Not this time and he staggers off to lick his wounds. My mother reaches for a small brown bottle and shakes out some pills. She swallows one of them and she sits there for the rest of the night, staring into space and not moving. The others make her a drink, talk to her, but she doesn't drink or speak. Finally, she gets up and slumps off to bed, taking the pills with her. I wonder why she takes those pills, as far as I can see, all they do is make her quiet. She used to talk, she used to tell us off and shout at us and I hated it then, but it was better than this. Her silence deafens me, but there's always the song on a loop to take its place.

It is a warm summer's day and I'm playing outside when the sight of his car makes my heart lurch. I freeze on the spot, staring ahead as he heaves himself out of the driver's seat and on to the street. His face is contorted with anger and I quake, thinking the anger is with me, that he will beat me to a pulp right here and now in the alleyway. The beast though staggers past, with his bad leg making him dip up and down, his purple face bobbing. My mother sees him and her face drops. She looks terrified and she picks up the baby and walks as quick as she can. He picks up the nearest object, a shovel, one of those old tin ones with a wooden handle, and he throws it at full force. It hits her square in the middle of her back and she crumples for a moment, the baby screaming up at her. She steadies herself and carries on walking until she's out of sight. He hobbles up the yard, but my brother has shut the door and he bangs in frustration. I slip slowly back into my own pool of invisibility and my father staggers away towards where my mother has run, with no hope of catching her. I ask myself, once again, 'Why are we so scared of someone who can't even run?' That night, my mam sits in her chair in the corner and the tears roll down her face, one after the other, but she doesn't wipe them away. I get some toilet paper and hold it out to her, but she doesn't see me. Her eyes are strange, they are open, but I'm sure she can't see.

I stand in the hallway with my back against the wall, staring at my own shoes. There is a lady, a stranger, sitting on her haunches in front of me. She looks quite young and she's wearing a flowery dress and a cardigan that looks like the one my mam knits. She holds my hands gently and looks directly, but kindly, into my eyes. She asks me a strange question about who I would choose to live with, my mam or my dad. I don't understand why she's asking me, no one has ever asked me anything like this before or taken any notice of what I think, that's why I'm quiet. But, as she's asked, the answer is easy. I'd rather live with my mam, I say, even though she doesn't talk and she's always sad, even though she never seems to be there, I'd rather live with her, because she doesn't scare me, not as much as he does anyway. The lady nods and writes something down in her notebook, then she asks the others the same. I go out to play and I see the lady walk away with her head down. She looks sad and I wonder how many other sad ladies there are in the world and will I be a sad lady when I grow up and what will happen next?

I'm watching 'Top of the Pops' with the others, banging on the arms of the chairs to the music, laughing, singing. A rare occasion when we're together, no threats, no shouting, no banging except for the banging of fists to the rhythm of the song. Then a louder banging overrides our banging. It's fists of a different kind, on the front door. 'Let me in, it's my name on that fucking rent book. I'll bang this bleeding door down in a minute, open it now or I'll smash the fucking window!' Then out of nowhere, serene as anything, my mother glides across the living room and down the lobby, like the figurehead on an ancient ship gliding through calm waters. Our mouths gape open and we can't believe it when, calm as you like, she opens the door and walks out 'They're all yours,' she says and without a backward glance, she manoeuvres around the bulk of the beast, suitcase in hand and disappears, blocked from view by the sheer size of him. Once he's got over the shock, he stands in the living room triumphant in his victory. He has won the right to return to 'his' house. After all, he reminds us, it's his name on the tenancy. Your mother, he tells us has 'ran off' with a new man with whom, the beast announces, she has been 'having it off with for months.' He continues with a tirade of insults aimed at our mam, then self-praise and justification of why we are better off with him. He tells us that he could have put all of us into care and, if it wasn't for him, that's where we would be. I know I'm not alone in wishing he had put us into care, anywhere would be better than here I think. I wish he would put us into care. Maybe they care about you in care. He tells us that from now on, we'll have decent food, not that shite she used to have in. I listen, but my instincts tell me not to get my hopes up.

I return from playing in the street and push open the door to the living room. He is on the big square vinyl chair near the fire and I can see that he is angry. He asks me where I've been and calls me a whore, asks me if that's where I've been, 'whoring.' I am nine years old and don't understand the meaning of 'whoring', only that it must be bad. I answer 'no,' but this only seems to make him more annoyed. He leaps up out of his chair and I feel the full force of his hand across my face. The power of the blow sends me flying and I land on the other side of the room. I slump against the wall and hold my nose which throbs with pain, but not as much as my heart which breaks a little more each day.

I'm playing at my friend's house in the best room. It's good here because they seem to really like me. My friend's Nanna says nice things to me, says I'm patient and kind, not like her granddaughter. She says it's good that her granddaughter has me to play with because I teach her how to be a good person. I never thought I was a good person. We're listening to L.P.s in the front room. Nancy Sinatra, 'These boots are made for walking'. We're having a good time. We sing along and march around the room, pretending to wear Nancy's white boots. We're dancing and laughing, holding on to each other and whirling around the room. Then there's a knock on the door and I know it's for me. My heart sinks. It's my sister, I need to go home now. Every time I'm having a bit of fun, I need to go home. It's as if he doesn't want me to enjoy myself. Reluctantly, I say goodbye, get my coat and walk back home. I push open the back door and he's there, standing over the cooker. "Get the pots washed," he says and I quickly hang up my coat and start the task. Just as I thought, nothing urgent, nothing that couldn't have waited. I'm sure one of the others could have washed up, it's not just my job, but this happens all the time. Just as I'm enjoying myself, he brings me back to where I don't want to be, back to this house.

For once in my life, my dad gives me some good news. He tells me that I've passed my eleven plus exam. He tells me that he always knew I was a 'clever bugger' and I think he looks pleased. I don't really know what to do, but I smile and I'm proud of myself because I know that not many people pass the eleven plus. My dad goes on to say that I passed 'with flying colours,' according to the Headmaster. When the others find out, they start to tease me, saying I'll be too good for them now that I'm going to Grammar School. Even though the teasing has already started, I'm still happy that I've done something good. I'm scared though, because I'll be the only one going to that school and I might not know anyone there. It's going to be murder at home now with the teasing. They already call me names which they shout out every time I try to be clever; 'little miss clever clogs,' 'know-it-all' and 'snobby pants.' One day I was talking to the cat, like we all do, 'are you feeling insecure?' I asked. I'd used a big word and that was the cause of great laughter and teasing. 'Who do you think you are?' they asked. 'No one,' I said. I begin to wish I'd never have taken that exam, I just want to be invisible again, to hide behind the settee where no one can see me. I want to disappear into a private place where I can read my books and be by myself.

We're on our way to the Co-Op to buy the uniform for Grammar School. We're walking through the store, past all the stalls. We're in the children's section where the school uniforms are, me and my big sister, Sylvia. She's seventeen now and she's taken time off work to take me shopping. When my dad isn't there, she takes charge and gets us all organised. I suppose she has become like the mother in our house. We all have nicknames and they call her 'milk round' because of her big chest. I look up at her now and that's all I can see. It's like a big round shelf sticking out. My nickname is 'snot rag' because I'm always wiping my nose on my sleeve. I wonder if I'll progress to 'milk round' one day. We're waiting for the lady to come back with my shirts, the last thing on the list. There's a pile of clothes on the counter and they're all for me. I can't wait to wear them in a couple of weeks' time, but I feel apprehensive because I know the teasing will only get worse, especially when they see me all dressed up in green. I know that I've made the right decision though, because it might help me get away. I want to get a good job so that I can leave home and make a life for myself. I don't want to end up like my mother. Every night when I go to bed, I hurt inside my chest. I don't really know why, but I think it's because I see my friends with their families and they seem happy. Their mums and dads don't hate each other and they get cuddles and hugs and kisses. I don't think my mum ever gave me a hug, my dad certainly didn't. So, when I have a family, I'm going to make sure they get lots of cuddles and hugs and kisses. I'm going to make sure they know that they're wanted and I'm going to make sure that I don't marry someone like my dad.

It's the first day at Grammar School and I'm dressed from head to toe in new clothes. I slip on the shiny black shoes, also free from the Co-Op, and walk around in them. They feel stiff and make my feet feel like wood. I can't walk properly and I think everyone will look at me when I get to school. I wonder if they'll know I've got free clothes and shoes on. I bet they will because I look so stupid in them. When I look in the mirror, there's a stranger looking back. Surely that's not me looking all neat and smart because inside I feel like a mess. I'm nervous about starting a new school, but I'm proud that I've made it, that I've been the only one in the family who is clever enough to pass that exam. As I walk up the path to the school, my stomach is churning and that song is in my head again. I think I'm going to be sick. I go up the stone step and through the big wooden door, then I'm met by a teacher who steps forward and smiles. She asks for my name and tells me not to be nervous and I wonder how she knows. She takes me into the hall to join the others for assembly. When it's over, we're shown to our class and we walk out to the prefab. I feel slightly better now we're in a smaller space. I look round the room and think that everyone looks so posh. I wonder if they think the same about me, with my new uniform on. Probably not because you can tell I'm not posh and I bet they can see right through me to the scruffy little kid inside who nobody wants to know. We're sent to line up for our dinner tickets and I join the queue. I'm embarrassed for what is to come because I'm 'free dinners' and they'll find out now. The way it works is that you bring you dinner money and get five tickets, one for each day. But I don't have any money because we can get free dinners, as well as the free orange juice and baby milk we get from the clinic every week. The queue has moved on and it's my turn. "I'm free dinners," I manage to mumble and I know they're all looking at me. The lady asks for my name and she ticks it off on the list. She hands me a strip of five tickets with FREE DINNER written across each one. Now everyone knows that I don't belong here, that I'm not like them. Even though my clothes are new, I feel like the scruffiest person alive. Another first day at school for little miss social misfit.

My sister has a sewing job at one of the local factories. She says it's boring but it pays well and they have a laugh sometimes. She asks me to come and meet her one day after school so I can see where she works and meet the girls. When I get there, she introduces me to the ladies on the shop floor and they fuss over me. 'Look at you in your new uniform,' 'you must be really clever to go there.' I feel awkward and proud at the same time. They give me a drink of cordial and a chocolate biscuit and I eat it hungrily because I'm starving after the walk from school. When we've said goodbye to the ladies, we walk home slowly, chatting about the day and I tell my sister about my music lesson, tell her that the teacher said I have a natural talent and I'm very good at it. She tells me well done and says I should become a singer and go on Top of the Pops. I tell her that I don't think I could ever sing on the stage in front of all those people. She tells me that she thought she would never be able to sew and that she was so nervous on her first day at work, but now she's one of the fastest machinists in the place. I'm glad for her and she's glad for me. When we get home, I'm first at the back door and I push it open slowly. That sinking feeling grips me and I don't see his hand, but I feel it hard on the side of my face and it stings. Still dazed, I look up to see the purple explosion that is my father's face. "You had the fuckin' key," he bellows at full volume. He had been 'stood there like a stork,' he says and had to get my little brother to climb through the pantry window. He looks so angry and I bet he couldn't wait to give my gormless little face a bashing when I finally got home.

It's my birthday today, I'm thirteen, a teenager and I've got a couple of cards from my sisters. I've been running errands for them, getting their supplies of sanitary towels, which are always put in a brown paper bag. I can understand why they always send me because it's embarrassing asking for them. I'm glad they wrap them up but I'm sure everyone knows what's inside the bag. The eldest sister always sends me for a quarter bottle of sherry on a Friday night from the 'Offy' by the canal, she says it gets her in the mood to go out. This also comes in a brown paper bag and I'm always scared of dropping it because I know she doesn't have much money and it's dear to buy sherry. She lets me sit with her sometimes while she puts her make-up on, and I'm always drawn to looking at that massive chest of hers getting in the way as she puts on her mascara. Later, she'll stagger in or, if she can't find her key, she'll throw stones at the bedroom window where me and my sister sleep in the bunks and we'll have to let her in, telling her to be quiet or my dad will hear us. Then we'll all be in trouble. Once, she climbed in through the back window and left her platform shoes in the yard. The dog from the corner shop ran off with one of the shoes and she had to go around the next day and ask for it back. She's always going out and getting drunk but my dad doesn't hit her though. I don't know why, but I think it's because she looks after us lot.

There's a boy in my class with big puppy dog brown eyes and floppy brown hair which hangs over the side of his face. He has a moustache that sits on his top lip and lovely white teeth when he smiles. He's a bit shorter than me as I've grown to be a 'lanky streak of piss,' so they all say. They call me Miss Biafra and say they can see my hip bones ten minutes before I appear because they stick out that much. I don't know why I'm so thin. There are times when there's not much food in the house, but I always have a free school dinner. It isn't my fault I'm bony and my friend's mum thinks I'm undernourished. God, I was mortified when I heard that. That explained why they invited me for tea. To fatten me up. Great. Anyway, my love for this boy in my class is predictably unrequited. It doesn't help that I'm scared of boys and find it almost impossible to talk to them without my face turning bright red. So, I resort to admiring him from a distance, mostly during Maths when we're in the same set and I can sneakily watch him from the other side of the room. I wish he would notice me but I don't think he will.

I'm out with some of the girls from school at a local pub-come-disco. It's noisy and lively and I feel uncomfortable, especially when I'm trying to dance because I'm not very good at it and I feel awkward with everybody looking at me. Standing in a circle and watching my friends giggle and chat makes me feel under pressure to contribute, but I don't know what to say. I open my mouth to say something, but I seem to have an automatic filter in my brain that tells me not to bother because nobody would want to listen to it. I desperately try to think of something interesting to say but go red in the face just anticipating my turn to talk, so I don't bother. I wish I could stop myself blushing, I wish I could be like my friends and be able to talk and dance without feeling stupid. I might not be able to dance and I might not be able to talk without blushing, but I can write and I can make people laugh. That gets me into trouble now and again, like when I made up poems about the teachers and passed them round in class. My friend had a laughing fit and got caught with the paper. The teacher's face was a picture when she read the poem, I'm sure she was hiding a giggle, but I got detention anyway. It was worth it though, just to make them laugh and think I was good at something. At least I felt like I could do something right. Once, the English Teacher read one of my stories out to the class and she said it was brilliant. I thought there was a note of surprise in Miss's voice. Did she not expect such a 'no-hoper' to do well? Anyway, slowly but surely, these little successes helped to build my confidence and make me believe that I do have a place in the world. One day, I'm going to leave school and get a good job. Then I'll be able to get away from that awful house and make a life of my own. I've already done the sums by asking what my sisters earn and by asking my brother how much rent he pays. I think I could manage, especially if I get a better job than my sisters. I will have to see if my dad lets me go to college. He's already told me not to get any smart ideas about it because I've got to earn some money, but we'll see. He might change his mind if I can convince him that I would earn more money in the future if he let me go to college. I could be a teacher if I'm clever enough. That would be my dream.

We're in his bedroom, having a cuddle on his single bed. In the middle of what seems like the longest kiss in history, he suddenly stops and looks at me intently. "I think it's time," he says. I've thought about this moment for a long time, about what I should do when it comes. Some of my friends at school have already done it, done 'the deed'. I wonder how they manage to look so normal. All I remember of 'the deed', if that's what it was, is the hurt, the shame, the stinging, not being able to walk properly and thinking that everyone knew. I wonder if he'll know when we decide to do it that I've already done it before. I wonder if he'll know that I'm not pure, not a virgin. I bet that he'll be able to tell, because I probably won't bleed. Then what will he think? He's older than me, he's nineteen, but he's nice to me. He's always telling me how beautiful I am, no one has ever said that to me before. He wants to marry me one day, he says, but I tell him I'm still at school and can't think about things like that, I'm too young, but inside I'm glowing. I decide that it is time; I'd rather it be him than someone else who isn't so nice and gentle. We kiss some more and he sucks hard on my chin, on my neck. He promises not to hurt me. We get undressed and I wonder if he'll laugh at my little pimples. 'Two Aspirins on an ironing board,' one of the boys at school called them. He doesn't laugh though, he looks at me with such love, such kindness. When it happens, it's not as bad as I thought it would be and I'm glad it was him, because I knew he would be gentle and careful. I lie there afterwards, staring at the ceiling, not really feeling anything, but I'm crying, sobbing and that song is going around in my head and it won't go away. Eventually, I tell him that I'd better go. He puts on the light and passes over my clothes, then a shocked expression takes over his face. "What?" I ask. 'Your chin has a massive bruise on it, I'm so sorry.' I look in the mirror and my chin is purple. 'He's going to kill me!' When I arrive home, my dad asks me where I've been and I tell him that I've been to my friend's house to listen to the new Osmonds album. 'Don't give me that shit, you lying little whore,' he snaps back. I hang my head because that's what I feel like, a lying little whore, but my dad wouldn't understand that I only slept with the boy because he was kind and I didn't want my 'first' time to be with someone who was going to hurt me. I don't think he understands anything except how to get to the pub and drink himself into oblivion. He certainly doesn't understand why I would want to go to college, he mustn't, because he's told me 'it's a load of crap' and 'you can go out to work and bring some money home.' So, that's what I've got to do. 'What's that love bite on your chin?' 'It's not a love bite, the bus jerked and I banged my chin on the bar,' I say, looking down at my shoes, not wanting him to see my lying eyes. A few months later, I end it with the boy who thought he'd taken my virginity. He is absolutely devastated and I feel really mean, but I want to move on because I feel stifled. Also, he's not got a job yet and I want a better life for myself. I want more than to get pregnant and settle for a council flat in Salford.

Months later, I'm in my rickety little wooden bed with a hairy blanket over my head. The tears won't stop and my face is a swollen mess. The song in my head is driving me mad, it won't go away. The lad I've been seeing for a few weeks has just ended it and I'm hurting so much that I don't think I'll ever stop crying or get out of bed. My sister comes into the bedroom and stands over me. 'What's the matter with you?' I peer out through the hairy blanket, 'Jed's finished with me. He says I'm too clingy and he doesn't want to be bogged down too young.' I'm all hot and snotty and I'm exhausted. My head feels like it's going to split open, what with the song and the pain. 'Never mind, there'll be others. Come on, it's tea time and my dad'll go mad if we don't go down. Go and wash your face and calm down. He thinks you're up here doing some ironing. He won't be happy if he knows you're crying over some boy.' I know she's right, that if I don't pull myself together and go downstairs, I'll just make things worse, so I splash my face and the cool water feels good.

I'm at Clive's house and his mum has asked me to stay for Sunday dinner. I love being here, where people talk to me and listen when I talk to them. I like the feeling of being part of a family, even though it's not my own. It's been hard, in a way, to realise that other families are different to your own. It makes me wonder why our family isn't like this, why my parents don't seem to care at all about us. I thought it was the same with everyone, but I've seen the way other parents look at their children, how they hug them and care about them. The smell coming from the kitchen is divine. I know I should really go home because I told my dad I was going to see my friend, Mary and if I stay out too long, he'll know I've lied, but the smell is so tempting that I agree to stay. The dinner is delicious, the best meal I've had in ages. Clive's family ask me questions about myself, so I tell them about all my brothers and sisters and about work, trying to make everything sound 'normal', like their family. I thank them for the lovely meal and tell them I have to go or else my dad will worry about me. Not much chance of that really. When I arrive home my dad is absolutely fuming. 'Where do you think you've been all day?' he booms. I step into the living room and find my voice, 'I've been at Mary's.' The loudest bellow comes from his mouth, 'Mary's? Mary's? I'll give you bleeding Mary's! You're nothing but a lying whore, just like your mother.' I don't understand how he knows I've been with a boy, but I'm scared of how angry he is so I don't say anything, just stand there looking at my shoes. 'Our Frank's coming to get you later, you can go and live with him out of my sight. I've had enough of you and your lies. Bleedin' Mary's. What a load of crap!' I'm a dithering wreck and I can't get any words out. 'At least I'll get away from here,' I think. I go upstairs and pack a bag, not that there's much to put in it. I sit with my pathetic hoard of belongings and wait for my brother to pick me up. 'You should have known what would happen if you stayed out,' he says when he arrives. 'I know but I was having a nice time at my friend's, that's all,' I answer, not wanting to think about what will happen to me now. 'He's not stupid you know. He knows where you've been. It's written all over your face. Anyway, you can stay in the spare room at ours until you find somewhere else to live, but don't think you'll be bringing boys back, there'll be none of that.' The room is in fact a tiny attic space, sparse and Spartan, but there is a little window from which I can view the world below and it's my own space. My brother has a girlfriend living with him so I don't think there will be any attention coming my way in that respect. For that I'm thankful, although I do feel like a bit of a spare part.

I carry on with my life, going to work and enjoying a big night out with my friend at weekends, normally Friday. I'm getting chatted up a lot and I genuinely don't understand why. I still have a feeling inside that everyone else is better than me even though my friends at school always told me I could be a model, so much so, that I went to see an agency once. They asked me to walk across the room and the lady pulled disapproving face as I did so. She said I didn't have good posture, so I didn't chase it up, just told my friends 'I told you so.' Apparently, I walk with a stoop, but I feel so tall and lanky and I don't want people to look at me. Three months later and a flat has become available downstairs from our Frank's. I'm glad, because, not only am I in the way of our Frank and his girlfriend, but I brought a lad home the other night and our Frank went beserk. "You! Piss off!" he said to the lad. I was so embarrassed. I was only making him a cup of coffee in the kitchen. Now I might not see him again and that's a pity, because he was a nice-looking lad. Why does everything have to go wrong, just when I think I've found someone who I like?

I knock on the big wooden door of the house at the other side of ours. After a little while, the landlady appears. She's very old, an ex-doctor's wife, very well-spoken and even though she's about eighty-three and as thin as a little bird, I'm a bit scared of her. "It's Frank's sister," I say. "Oh yes, Frank told me about you," she says, "just let me get the key and I'll show you round. The rent will be thirteen pounds a week payable every Monday, starting this Monday. It's got a nice big bedroom and your own kitchen. Is that alright for you?" I do a quick calculation. That'll leave six pounds out of my wages. "That's fine," I say. The main living room in the flat is huge with a massive bay window and a high ceiling. There's only a tiny gas fire to heat the whole of the space and that's seen better days. There are draughts coming in from the windows and under the doors, but I'm sure it'll be alright. She tells me I can move in on Sunday if I want and I agree. My first taste of freedom. I set about making the flat more comfortable and homely, starting with a coat of paint and the addition of some plants which were hastily bought without much consideration or knowledge. Two wicker baskets containing ivy which trails its green leaves down the wall in contrast to the white background. It looks quite striking and it gives me a sad little thrill to know it's all my own work. I can make this place my own and it feels good.

A few weeks later, I've just got in from work and there's a knock at the door. I jump out of my skin, a knee-jerk reaction, a travesty of my former life. When my heart stops thumping in my chest, I wonder if one of the other tenants has locked themselves out, but when I pull the door back I get the shock of my life, because there stands my dad, looking angrier than ever, with our Gail, my younger sister next to him. She is standing with her head down, a large bag by her side. "She can come and live with you, I've had enough of her. I'll send a tenner into school every week with your brother." Before I can protest, not that it would do any good at all, he turns on his heel and manoeuvres awkwardly down the front steps, swinging his 'bad' leg round with each forward movement. He looks a sorry sight but I'm absolutely terrified of him, even though he now has little control over my life. I take Gail by the arm and help her in with her bag, guiding her to the lumpy settee. We sit and hug for a while in front of the gas fire, just staring into it as if looking for inspiration. We share the same history. We're very different, but we share the same history, with the same outcome. "I hate him!" are her first words, when she finds them. "So do I," I say, "he doesn't care about anyone but himself. Fancy chucking you out at fifteen and expecting me to look after you. What kind of a father would do that to his daughter? Well, we both know the answer to that don't we? I'll do my best Gail, you know that, but I'm just so angry at him, the ignorant, arrogant git. As soon as we're too old to get the family allowance, we're out on our arse. Ah well, at least we didn't get pregnant like the others, I suppose we can be thankful for that." She looks up then, "I never want to see him again!" she says. "Well, you don't have to. You'll be leaving school soon and you can get a job like me. We'll be fine, we don't need him or her. She doesn't give a shit either. Can't even be bothered to make us a cup of tea when we go around. Well, we can look after ourselves now and do a better job than they ever did."

Gail settles in, a little too well, if you ask me. She establishes a good social life, as young as she is, and enjoys a Monday night out at a local club which runs a disco aimed at younger people, not as young as Gail, but she does look about nineteen, so she gets away with it. The next few months are spent working and making sure Gail gets to school on time. It's exam time and I'm trying to make sure she knows the importance of education as a way out. Not that it's ever helped me as I wasn't allowed to take it further, but I know I won't be stuck in this job forever. My dad sends ten pounds with my brother to school every week and this helps to pay the rent, but as soon as Gail finishes school, she'll have to find a job, just like I did. The girls I work with don't have this problem, they live at home quite happily and it strikes me how lucky they are to have such great parents. We've always looked after each other and ourselves with little parental input, or so it seemed to us. Now, I'm playing the role of mother to my younger sister and it's a big responsibility because I can see her going 'off the rails.' She's already been involved in a fight on her way home one Monday and her choice in boyfriends leave a lot to be desired. She did meet a decent boy once, but she finished with him and the reason she gave was that he was 'too nice.' I think she likes a bad boy, but they're not for me. I like to know where I stand and I like to be treated well. I don't want to end up like my mam, having to dodge fists and insults all the time and not having time for your own kids. I want a different life than that.

CHAPTER 8

James
2017

James closes the door, takes a deep breath and sits in the armchair opposite his therapist. He's been here before, but not for a while.

"Good to see you again James."

"I'd like to say the same, but, you know."

"Yes, I know, you wouldn't be here if everything was great, would you?"

"No."

"So, what's been happening? What brings you here again?"

James shuffles in his seat. He doesn't know where to start. He's been reflecting a lot recently.

"Well. Something's happened that's made me look at things differently."

"Not always a bad thing, but, go on."

"It's Alison, she's turned up again."

"I see."

"It's brought everything back. I'm not proud of the way I've handled things in the past. I'm ashamed really."

James hangs his head and Doreen passes him a tissue. He blows noisily into it.

"Sorry. It's just a bit overwhelming."

"Never apologise for showing your feelings James. Take your time."

"I'm alright, really, it's just that I wanted to talk things through so I could get to grips with how I'm feeling. I need to be strong and I need to try to understand."

Doreen didn't respond, she wanted to give James time to think about what he wanted to say next, what he wanted to disclose. Eventually, James started to talk and, once he started there was no stopping him. He revisited the main events which had shaped his life and which had brought him here again.

"…and now she's reappeared and it feels like I've had the wind punched out of me, just like I did when I first met her, but not in a good way this time. That first time I saw her, she just stood out from the others, you know. She was tall, yes, but she had this kind of innocent beauty about her, this kind of 'little girl lost look'. I wanted to care for her, to look after her and I failed. I failed so badly, but I was young and so was she and………"

"Take a minute James."

"Sorry."

Doreen gave him a mock warning look and they both smiled. James regained his composure and carried on.

"I just want to make things right. I know I can't go back and change things, I know I've got to move forward, but I feel like I've got this heavy weight in my chest holding all the guilt inside and I don't know how to make it go away."

Doreen smiled at him. She didn't need to say anything. James had to work it out for himself.

"When I saw her face again, all those memories came rushing back………"

CHAPTER 9

Marriage, Birth and Decline
1981

It's a nice spring evening and my sister and I are getting ready to walk down to the pub where we can spend some of our hard-earned wages and let go a bit. We've both started a waitressing job in the evenings. It's hard work, but it means that Gail has some money of her own, she needs it the way she knocks the cider back. She's still only fifteen, but she's what they call 'well-developed' and probably looks older than me. We're as different as chalk and cheese. Her nickname is Bridget because she looks like an Irish girl with her red cheeks and curly black hair. My hair is fair and my skin pale. Where she has curves, I have slight mounds. My nickname has progressed from 'snot rag' to 'flutes', due to my long, thin body with hardly any chest or bum to speak of. At least I have a hope of filling out now that I've left home and I'm in control of my own food.

I finish off my make-up with another layer of mascara and, I must admit, my eyes look great. I think they're my best feature by far as, let's face it, nothing much else stands out about me. Gail has the ample cleavage, as young as she is. Just like our elder sister, she seems to be like a magnet to the boys.

"Are you nearly ready?" I call and she pops her head around the kitchen door.

"Two shakes of a donkey's tail," she says.

She makes me laugh half the time with all her quirky sayings, the other half she frustrates me to hell.

"Come on, let's go, the love of your life might be waiting in the Hare and Hounds."

"Yeah, like hell, more like the son of Frankenstein," she replies.

Finally, we leave the flat and walk into town, Gail holding her head rigid so as not to spoil her hair do, which is going nowhere since it's secured in place with about a hundred clips. We always walk to save on bus fares, because, after the food shopping, there isn't much left. However, despite out lack of funds, we need to go out at weekend or else we'd go mad. It's great to have work but it's hard to get up every day and do a boring job, especially when it's cold. You can see your breath in that flat and we've had to put cling film on the windows to keep out the draught. That little fire is less than useless. Sometimes, there's nothing else we can do but go to bed early so we can at least try to stay warm under the covers.

We have our first half of lager and black in the Hare and Hounds, savouring the sweet liquid which feels like a great reward after a long week. We chat with others that have become familiar faces, then we move on to the next pub. There are loads of pubs in Eccles, but we have our favourites. We're getting to know the regulars a bit now and it's nice to have a bit of banter with them. I still have that thing about not wanting to talk sometimes, I can't quite believe that anyone would want to listen to me.

Gail more than makes up for it though, and I probably meet more people because of her. She always starts the chat. She's loud and a bit cheeky to my quiet and shy.

We're back in the Hare and Hounds now and she's laughing at the bar with some young lad.

"Cheer up love, it might never happen," the person next to me says.

I look around and see the face of an unfamiliar lad. I blush and wish Gail would hurry up back. Finally, she returns and I take my drink before she has chance to put it down on the table.

"Bloody hell love, you were desperate for that weren't you?" the man next to me says.

"Not bloody much," pipes up Gail and we do a quick 'cheers' and finish off half of our drinks in one go, then we go to find a table.

There's only one free, so we squeeze in along the vinyl bench along the back wall. The men around the table look like they've had a few more than us and it's not long before we decide to move on. These blokes are much older than us, but they seem to have taken a bit of a shine to Gail. We stand and edge our way out, but just as I turn around, I bump into someone and he spills his pint down my lovely new top. When I look up, a blonde lad with a massive grin is apologising and offering to buy me a drink.

"You're alright, we're going now," I reply, trying to keep my voice steady so as not to betray my frustration at having my best top ruined.

He looks disappointed.

"I'm sure I've seen you before," he says and I give him a puzzled look.

"No, honestly, it's not a chat-up line, I think you were at that party in Clifton a couple of weeks ago."

I look at him carefully, then the penny drops. "Oh yeah, you came on a motorbike didn't you? I remember you walking in with your helmet on and wondering who you were," I say.

"That was me! I'm James. I'm a friend of Steve's, whose party it was. Look can I take you out for a drink? At least let me do that so I can make up for the one I've just spilt down you."

I don't really know what to say but I quickly write down my number and hand it to him, conscious of Gail waiting to go, although, looking at her, she seems to be getting on well with his mate. By the time we stagger home late that evening, we're both very pleased with ourselves, having both given our number to the guys in the pub. 'They've got to call us yet,' I remind Gail, but she says she's not that bothered anyway, they weren't that good-looking. I laugh with her, but secretly, I'm pleased to have caught someone's attention and I'm hoping against the odds that he'll call me.

The call finally comes on the Tuesday night, after three days of wondering if he meant what he said and if he liked me at all. We arrange to meet the following night and I manage to borrow a decent outfit to wear, having worn my 'best' one at the weekend when we met. Once I get dressed the nerves kick in and the self-doubt starts. 'What if he only found me attractive because he'd had a few drinks? What if he doesn't turn up? What if he does turn up but then he turns back and walks away when he sees me?' I'm sure he was half cut when we met and he didn't see me properly. I bet he'll be disappointed when he sees the size of my chest and how thin I am. I don't care what they say about the likes of Twiggy, men seem to want curvy girls and I've got a lot of growing to do.'

My fears are soothed when he greets me with a broad and welcoming smile, compliments me on my outfit and takes my hand. The pub we choose is quiet, but not empty and we enjoy a pleasant evening of chat and laughter. He tells me about his family, which consists of his mum, step-dad and half-sister, with a couple of grans who he has regular contact with. I hesitate when it comes to talking about my own so-called parents, but decide that he should know about my circumstances from the start. He's sympathetic about my past and visibly angry when I tell him about my father.

"Don't let me meet him, I'd want to knock his lights out," he says and I reply that it's highly unlikely that their paths would cross as, for obvious reasons, we no longer have contact.

We arrange to meet again the following week and our relationship develops after a bit of a shaky start. He was late for the second date and I thought he wasn't coming. The more I thought about it, the more worked up I was and, because I was upset, the date didn't get off to a very good start. Once he'd explained the traffic situation though, I felt better. He said I would understand when I learned to drive and saw how busy the roads were. He's a bit older than me, at twenty, and he's able to borrow his mum's car, so he's quite used to being stuck in traffic, especially on the motorway.

On our third date we go to Lymm. I've heard it's a

nice little village but I've never been. Once we're there I feel out of my depth, like everyone is looking at me and judging me, that familiar feeling that people can see right through to my core and know that I'm not like them. They seem so aloof, like they're from another world and it makes me feel inadequate. They seem 'snobby' and pretentious to me and in contrast I feel common and scruffy. James laughs it off but I don't think he realises how uncomfortable I am in this environment. Everyone appears to be so confident, smug even. Some of the girls are stunning and I think James is beginning to regret having me here. I think I just saw him craning his neck to look at the backside of one of them and this does not help my mood at all. There's a very awkward interlude before he asks me what's wrong. He seems incredulous and a little bit affronted when I suggest he's eying that blonde girl up, but I just think 'he would deny it wouldn't he.'

The whole scenario builds up into a bit of a nightmare and I just want to go home. It makes me doubt whether I want to get involved in the world of dating at all, but, at the end of the eventing, when he asks could he see me again, I don't hesitate to agree.

Over the next few months, we become physically and emotionally close and before long we talk about the future. It's an exciting time but very unsettling for me, as I seem to swing from being completely sure of his love to doubting it for one reason or another. The roller-coaster of emotions is hard to deal with, but it's worth it to have someone who cares about me, who loves me. I've never experienced this before, maybe that's why it's difficult for me to get to grips with. It reminds me of the time I went to my friend's house and her mum went to hug me. She said I was as stiff as an ironing board and to relax as she wasn't going to bite. She didn't bite, but I remember feeling very awkward and not knowing what to do. Maybe there's an art in accepting love and hugs that I haven't yet learned.

It's Monday morning and I'm taking my ring into work to show the others. It's all wrapped up in its little box and shiny black plastic bag and when I open it up, there are gasps and admiring inspections. They hold it up to the light to see it sparkle, but when they hand it back to me, a couple of them are not smiling and I wonder why. It could be that they're envious of the ring, or they think I'm too young, but I know what I'm doing. I'm eighteen, but a mature eighteen, I like to think. He's twenty-one, so that's all right, he's a fully-grown man. There are plenty of people around who married young and are still happy and they weren't half as in love as we are, so I reckon we'll be just fine. Nothing is going to burst my bubble of joy. The only thing that would destroy me is if he leaves me. I think about this often, maybe too often to be healthy, but I can't help it. Now though, I can just look at my ring and I know that he will be here forever.

I can't remember ever being hugged by my mother, let alone really loved, but here I am, at her house, waiting for the wedding car. To say we're not close is a bit of an understatement. I've never really felt that she's been a real mother to us, she's become more like an acquaintance, someone I have a duty to see now and again but I don't really know why. After she left, my sister tried to arrange visits, but it was a whole year before we saw her again, which, in equal measure, angered my sister and broke her heart. She practically begged her to see us but was continually presented with one excuse after another, until my mother finally relented and agreed to see us. The visit was an anti-climax, her greeting being 'you don't want cups of tea do you?' It was as if she couldn't even be bothered to lift the kettle, raise an arm in greeting or even raise an eyebrow for these children she'd long since abandoned. Now we have reached, not forgiveness, but a mutual understanding that our relationship will never be more than this; two acquaintances rubbing shoulders now and again with awkward bouts of conversation. This morning is no less awkward, uneasy is the understatement. Frank's here, but instead of supporting me on my wedding day, he's going on about how 'spoilt' my husband-to-be is.

"Fancy getting a brand-new car for your twenty-first, I got a kick up the arse and back to work."

I don't respond to my brother's comments because there is no reasoning with him. I know it seems unfair to my brothers and sisters that a child can be so 'spoilt' by his parents, but he's an only child and I think his dad's quite well-off. His family is certainly worlds apart from mine, but he loves me and that's what matters. I'm so happy to have this chance of normality, to have a wedding day with a white dress, bridesmaids, a church, a cake, a meal and a man who loves me, no lump in sight. I'm happy that I didn't use pregnancy as an escape, not that I blame my sisters at all; it was the only way out they could see. Now, I'm going to have as much of a chance of a good life as other people do and I can't wait.

Frank will give me away. Frank who took it away will give me away.

The car arrives and Frank holds his arm up for me to link him. I'm shaking inside my white lacy dress, still scared of him, stomach churning, hands sweating. I link my arm into his and feel like that little girl, like I'm his property and he still has control. That song is there again, going around in my head, over and over again. I'm feeling like the dirty little girl-whore who lets people do wicked things. Song on a loop in my head and the world in front of me spinning.

"Whatever's the matter Alison?" I hear my mother say and I reply that it's nothing, I'm just nervous.

We step out and there's a few ladies outside my mum's front door, some of her older friends. They throw confetti and I tell them to stop,

"Stop it! Tell them to stop it!"

I put my head down and climb into the car, shaking from head to toe. There are no words. I want to look perfect but I feel dirty and now the ladies have ruined my perfect white look. My mood has changed and I need pull myself together before I get to the church, so I think about the smiling faces that will greet me there. I think about my sisters, brothers and friends, then I take a few deep breaths and I feel a lot better.

I cry at my own wedding, at the words of the vows. To love and honour, until death us do part. Those words make me feel safe, like nothing can get me now.

Someone is going to look after me, someone who loves me more than anything else and it feels good, but a little overwhelming. I look at my new husband and it doesn't matter that his mother is looking down her nose at me and my family. It doesn't matter because he's done it now, he's married me. He's married me, Alison, the common girl from Eccles, the one with the big family and a mother who left them, a father who drinks. How awful, how bloody awful that he chose me when he could have had his pick of posh Urmston girls, or even someone from bloody Lymm. It doesn't matter now because I am going to show all of you that money or so-called class doesn't make you happy, it's who you are and what you can offer that matters. I'm a nice person and I'm worth as much, if not more, than anyone else because I have a good heart. This is my mantra, the words I need to repeat to myself when I have doubts, when I'm in that pit of depression, 'feeling sorry for myself'. I know that feeling sorry for yourself doesn't get you anywhere, but sometimes I just cannot snap out of it, despite people telling me to all the time. Sometimes, I even feel that it would be better to die than battle with my thoughts every day.

Later, after the wedding breakfast, I am reluctant to circulate around the 'other' side. My own family presents enough of a challenge as far as personalities are concerned, but at least I know them, know they are on my level. The 'others' are a different matter. I think of them as way above me, even though I know that it's only money that sets us apart. Or is it? They seem to have neat little families who stay together and who care about each other, that's how it seems to me. When I look at the sea of faces on the other side of the room, where his family are, I see smiles, easy chatter and loving glances. I see them as a different breed and I look on them with envy. It strikes me how different our lives have been, his and mine, and how inferior I feel, but why should I feel inferior when none of it was my fault? I know that my

129

thoughts are irrational, that everyone is born the same, we are all on the same planet and made of the same stuff, but I can't shake this feeling that I'm still that scruffy little kid who is part of a seedy secret.

"Hello Alison, you look miles away there."

It's his mother, looking down her elegant nose at me, her beautiful chiffon attire mocking my sub-standard dress, the one I bought from a department store sale, not a select boutique. Even on my wedding day, when I know I look good, on the inside I feel like second-hand goods.

"Oh, you made me jump then. I was just thinking how nice everyone looks." Why do I always feel like what I am saying is inane and pointless? Why does she make me nervous?

"Yes, we scrub up well don't we?" she says, then off she goes, back to her group of friends, her 'ladies who lunch,' her drinking buddies.

Her sharp departure somehow serves to deflate me, but I'm determined not to be sad on this of all days, so I seek out my husband and spot him at the bar with a couple of his mates. As I approach, they're laughing out loud and I'm sure I hear them mention a girl's name, someone James used to see before he met me, but they suddenly fall silent when they see me, which doesn't help my mood at all.

"Here she comes, the beautiful bride," one of them says and I smile at them, but I no longer want to join them.

"Which one of you is going to buy me a drink?" I say, hoping they don't think me a bit forward or cheeky.

"Are you not looking after your missis James? Get her a drink lad and get me one while you're there."

130

James looks at me in a puzzled way, wondering, no doubt, why I'm seeking out a drink so early in the day. I'm wondering the same. I follow him to the bar and stand next to him, slip my hand into his just as he pulls it up to attract the attention of the barmaid. I feel stupid, but I swallow the tears which threaten to rise.

"It's all right, I've still got some Cava left on the table, I'll go and see if I can find it."

James gives me a quick nod, to let me know he's heard what I said, then carries on with his drinks order. I feel lower than ever, so I return to the table, find the Cava and drink it quickly so that I might feel a quick buzz of something. Happiness?

"Bloody hell our kid, you knocked that back didn't you," my brother says and I'm suddenly back to where I know, where I feel comfortable, where I know I'm on an equal footing.

"Yes, I needed that. Are you enjoying yourself?"

"Course I am, how could I not? It was a great meal and it's a lovely place. They're a bit posh, his family, though aren't they?"

"Yeah, a bit posh for the likes of us, but never mind, it's not them I've married, it's James and he's not posh at all."

"Don't you be too sure our kid, they're all posh and they all stick together. I've seen the way they look at us, like we're tramps."

"Don't be daft, we're all the same, we all come from the same place," I say, but I know my brother is right and I know I'll have to fight for my place in this new family, I'll have to prove myself as worthy. My priority now though, is to enjoy the best day of my life, the start of my life as someone who fits in.

In the months following the wedding, I am almost consumed by the need to have a baby. It governs my every thought and deed. Sensible people tell me to wait, to enjoy the time we have together first. They say we're still young and there's plenty of time, but it's all I can think of and I feel ready. It takes almost a year for me to persuade James that the time is right but, once he agrees, I get pregnant straight away and I'm delighted. I couldn't have asked for a better twenty-first present. We tell his mum and dad but she's not pleased at all and tells us that she won't be minding the child as it was our choice to have one so young, so we need to deal with it. I don't really care about that, I'm just glad I can have children. There's a woman at work who has spent years trying, but it hasn't happened. She is a lovely lady, but she's so very sad.

The pregnancy is uneventful and I work up to seven months, then spend two months at home preparing for the birth. When the time comes, we grab the hold-all which has 'lived' in the corner of our bedroom for two months and James drives to the local hospital with a nervous grin. I'm beyond excited, even though the pains take my breath away.

"Hello love, I believe it's your first child," says the midwife when she finally appears.

"Yes, it is. I'm getting contractions about every two minutes," I say.

"Well, you don't look as if you are," she responds and I wonder what I should look like.

"Come through and we'll examine you, but I think we'll be sending you home."

I lie back while she examines me, thinking we must have got it wrong.

"Blummin' eck, you're half way there," she says, looking astonished.

I feel faint and I'm scared that I'm going to pass out, so I try to sit up.

"Stay there love, I'll get you some water," she says.

I manage the whole labour on gas and air as, by the time I need something stronger, it's too late. Five hours after we arrive, our beautiful daughter is born and my first words are, "She's perfect." She has a tiny 'button' nose, blonde matted hair, pink cheeks and a 'rosebud' mouth. Her fingers are long and they wrap around mine as she sleeps. I cannot take my eyes off her and for the first few hours at least, I'm in a state of Euphoria, unable to sleep or think about anything else but this tiny bundle. I think I will burst with love.

"Put that child down," says my mother-in-law on her first visit.

I don't respond. I will hold my child all I want. When I hold my baby, I feel like I can take on anything.

"I cleaned your fridge, there was mould on the rubber around the door," she says.

My heart sinks. Why can't she be happy for us? It's not as if we've asked her for anything. She's made it clear that she won't be offering help, probably as punishment for being so young and stupid. I don't respond to this comment either. She holds the baby, Laura we have called her, and she does look pleased to see her, at least.

"She looks just like you James when you were a born, the same little nose," she says.

James grins that wide grin and he looks like the happiest dad on Earth.

Three days later, we take Laura home. It's nearly Christmas, but our days are spent washing nappies which we fish out of plastic buckets with wooden tongues and transfer to our old twin-tub washer. I adapt easily to motherhood for these first few months, but then things change. The criticisms are starting to get to me. It's either James wondering what I do all day or his mother wondering how on Earth I get the time to be 'down'. I start to doubt myself, feel that everyone is against me. I try going to mother and toddler groups, but the things these mums talk about don't interest me. I don't want to spend an hour talking about cooking batches of food and labelling them for the freezer. I don't want to see how happy the others are and how well they're coping. I come away feeling more lonely and isolated, more doubtful about my abilities as a mum.

Every day is the same. Get up, feed the baby, get dressed, go out for a walk with the pram. Same place, same shops, then back home. Most days, I feel like I'm going through the motions. I don't understand what's happening. I wanted this baby so much and now I'm miserable. Every day I tell myself that I'll feel better after a good sleep, but I never do. Sometimes my thoughts are the only words I have and so I feel like I'm living inside my head. I torture myself with thinking about what James is up to at work, how many young girls work there, does he talk to them? When he comes home, it's always the same. He asks about my day, I tell him the same things over and over, we eat tea, then the evening is taken up with the baby, with bathing and feeding and hushing and shushing and leaving and checking, then sleeping. The passion, the desire for each other has gone. When it does happen, it's a chore, for me at least. I want it to be over with quickly so I can go to sleep. The same old cycle every day until I think I'm going mad. When I suggest I look for a job, go back to work part-time, James is not pleased, neither is his mother. They both feel that a mother should be with her child and, as I wanted this so badly, I should be happy in the role, it should be enough. But, I'm ashamed to say, it isn't and I feel like I'm losing my sanity.

I'm like a monochrome version of my former self; dull, lifeless and tired. The tears come randomly, when I'm feeding the baby, cooking, walking or sitting and staring. Always the tears. I wipe them away, but they keep coming. The tears and the cotton wool head and the song going around and around in a loop.

It gets so bad that I no longer want to play with my child. I don't even want to talk to her. I push her around in her pram, hoping the fresh air will awaken something in me, but I am just as miserable when I get back home. Four O'clock is Postman Pat time. She jiggles about to the theme tune, but it makes my heart sink. Every day the same. Every day a few more cells in my miserable body give up the ghost. Every night I tell myself it will be better tomorrow, but tomorrow comes and I'm just the same. The same effort to get dressed, the same irritation, the same feeling of being in a black pit. The same dead limbs and dull mind. The same me. I wish I could morph into someone else, wish I could take out my brain and put it in a glass next to my bed, like people do with teeth, then next morning put it back in and things are how they used to be.

CHAPTER 10

Breaking the Shackles
1985

I pull the duvet tightly around my ears to block out the sounds of a household that carries on without me. I'm cocooned in my nest of oblivion. If I can't hear them, they can't see me. I know I've got a child to tend to, but I can't muster the strength to get up. What if I don't get up? I don't ever want to get up again. I'm rubbish at being a mum and I've let everyone down. My head is splitting in two and it's stuck to the pillow like a magnet, that bloody song going around and around in a loop. I wish it would just go away instead of reminding me all the time that 'this could be the last time.' I wish it was the last time! I can't face another day, can't face pretending to be happy and normal, when I know everyone is talking about me. He thinks I'm a failure, so does his precious mother, and who can blame them?

The door opens and my stomach flips. I don't want to speak to anyone. I just want to be left alone until my head feels better.

"You'd better get up Alison, we're going to mum's in a bit. Come on, you can't expect me to do everything when I've been at work all week."

I want to answer, I want to make everything better, but

I can't. The tears flow and my throat constricts. The vice around my head tightens. Song on a loop. Where the hell is that song coming from? 'This could be the last time, this could be the last time, maybe the last time, I don't know'. Competing with the song in my head, I can hear my husband muttering something about doctors but I can't move so I just lie there and cry. He'll do a better job than me anyway, I might as well just stay here. I pull the cover up over my head and hold it tightly, willing him to go away and he does.

When I wake up it's dark. I can hear pots being put away. My head is still splitting but I manage to get out of bed. My legs wobble underneath me and I sit on the bed until I feel steady enough to stand. I edge down the stairs like an old woman.

"I'm sorry," I whisper and I stand there feeling like a child in my own house.

Feeling judged and owned and controlled and useless. The tears come again.

"You look awful," he says.

'I already knew that,' I think.

"I'm sorry," I say again.

I seem to be saying sorry a lot these days.

"You're in at the doctor's tomorrow, ten o'clock."

I slump in the chair. I don't know what to say to him.

"Where's Laura?"

"Where do you think she is? She's in bed, it's nine o'clock. My mum wasn't very happy when you didn't come, says she can't understand it. I told her, that makes two of us. It's not like it's the 'baby blues' is it? She's nearly three for God's sake. I mean, you sit there, or lie there without saying a word, just crying. God knows what you've got to cry about. You've got the house, the husband and the child. You wanted them all. Now you've got them and all you can do is cry. I don't know how much more of this crap I can take."

I look at him and see how his face is changing again. The anger is coming. If I say I'm sorry again, he'll say he's sick of hearing sorry. If I don't say anything, he'll get frustrated, so I just sit and I hang my head. Damned if I do, damned if I don't. My head is in that vice again and I let my husband drag me back upstairs and slump me on to the bed and cover me up and slam the door. I let him do that because I don't know what else I can do.

The doctor looks up and swivels round in his chair.

"How can I help you today?"

I've lost my voice again. The tears come.

"Oh dear. Is there anything in particular making you feel like this?"

I shrug my shoulders. He asks a few questions then about housework, interests, sex life. He must think I'm so ignorant because all I can muster is 'I don't really know.' Then he asks about my relationship with my parents.

"I don't really have one," I say.

"Relationship or parent," he responds with a smile, then the floodgates open and I can't stop sobbing and shaking and that song on a loop in my head and I just stare at the doctor and he looks shocked. He mentions something about in-patient care and I just want to go back to bed!

I get my wish, to go back to bed. The bed is high and hard with a metal head board. I feel detached from my body which is stuck to the mattress like a big sack of potatoes that ache and are as lazy as you like. Strangely, I feel at peace. I don't have anyone telling me to get up, don't feel guilty for not tending to Laura, she isn't here so I can't do anything about it. The song is no longer in my head, just distant, incoherent voices which rise and fall and dip in and out of my consciousness. Next to my bed is a wooden locker, on top of which sits a small plastic cup and a plastic jug of water. I'm thirsty but my arms feel like iron and I don't think I have the strength to reach over. Tears which I don't ask for seep out. The voices disappear, replaced by a loud hum and I can feel myself drifting off.

My slumber is disturbed by someone shaking me.

"Can you sit up for me Alison?"

A nurse looms over me with a kindly look. My response is irritation. She is speaking to me like I'm two or maybe ninety-two. I sit up without meeting her gaze and she plumps up the pillows behind my back. That settles it then, I must be ninety-two.

"We've got an appointment for you later with a lovely lady who's going to talk things through with you and make a plan."

"Great."

"Take these, then we'll get you up and dressed."

She hands me the pills and I swallow them obligingly with the tepid water. They stick in my throat along with all the words I always mean to say but can't. Eventually they go down and I throw back the covers and swing my legs around to one side of the bed.

"Steady young lady, you'll come to grief doing that. Take it easy."

But before I have computed her words, I'm up on my feet, my legs wobbling and vision blurred, until I stumble and I have to accept her help to get me back on to the bed. I'm a twenty-four-year-old stuck inside a ninety-two-year-old's body, with no clear viewpoint to the future. Like an old person, I feel my life is all but done. I'm frustrated beyond belief, but other emotions are there too; relief that my child is being looked after properly. I'm thankful that she doesn't have to look at a useless mother every day, taunted by my presence but not benefitting from any maternal love. I'm grateful that she can have the chance of a life without me. That's when I decide. As soon as I get out of here, I'm off. It's the best thing I can do for everyone. I'm going to go away, as far as I can and leave my husband and child to get on without the burden of this useless ghost-being who just glides around the house looking on, but not able to participate. The irony that I am following the same path as my own mother who has so spectacularly messed up my life is not lost on me, but I don't have the energy to change it.

The nice lady comes to see me the next day, as promised.

"I'm going away," I tell her.

"Going away?"

"Yes, I've decided, it's no use pretending, I'm a crap

141

mother and everyone will get along so much better without me. I can't see an end to all this, so I need to end it."

"Is that how you really feel Alison, that everyone would be better off without you?"

"Yes. I just bring everyone down. I can't help it."

"That's why we're here, to help."

"By giving me pills? No thanks, I'd rather get away, make a new start where I'm not somebody's crap mother or wife."

"The treatment we offer is designed to get you through this hopelessness that you feel, until you can manage without them. There's no shame in it."

"There's no shame in taking pills, my shame comes from knowing everyone is looking at me and thinking what a rubbish mother I am, what a useless wife. My husband thinks I'm dull and I might as well not be here at all for all the good I do my child."

She knows I'm right. She's looking at me, trying to think what to say next, but she knows I'm right. I feel slightly better now that I've made a decision. I know it's the right thing for me and everyone else.

"When you came into hospital Alison, you agreed to a line of treatment which would involve both drug therapy and the help of a psychologist. The combination of these two could make a massive difference to the way you are looking at life."

"Maybe they could, but they're not going to change who I am. I'm a messed-up fucking mess who nobody ever wanted. I should never have had a child of my own, I'm not even capable of looking after myself!"

"What's the thing you're most proud of?"

"Passing my eleven-plus."

"How difficult was that?"

"I don't know, I never really thought about it, it just happened. I took the exam and I passed. Then someone mentioned I was in the top five percent in the country and I thought 'wow' because I never thought I was clever."

"Why do you think that was?"

"Because everyone seemed to be better than me. I always felt different."

"We can help you with that Alison, help you to become more confident."

"I don't need help. I don't want to take tablets that will turn me into a zombie, that I might get hooked on."

"Is that your fear?"

"No, it's not a fear, I'm not scared. I know what I have to do but I'm really tired now and I need to sleep."

"That's probably the best thing you can do for now. I'll leave you to rest and I'll be back tomorrow to see how you feel."

She gathers her papers and leaves the ward. She can come back tomorrow, but she won't find me here.

When I return home, I feel like even more of a stranger. I can't connect with anyone, nor do I want to. The conversations I have with myself, in my head, are endless. I talk myself into and out of doing things that might make me feel better, but everything seems like too much trouble. I no longer voice my thoughts, just sit here looking at life through gauze.

Each day begins and ends with struggle. Those debates which happen in my headspace begin as soon as I awake. I fight the lethargy, make this sack of useless bones get up and do what it is I must do. It's becoming increasingly difficult to leave my nest, where I can rest my aching head.

There is a child who I must chivvy through each day, so when I finally drag myself out from the comfort, I go to her because that's what I need to do. I go through the motions of being a mother without feeling anything but numbness. I know I should be enthralled by everything about her, but I just want my duties to be done so I can crawl back into my invisible mind space. I shuffle around the kitchen like a zombie, like someone who is only half-alive, the fog in my headspace making everything blurred. When she is fed, I slip on my coat over tea-stained pyjamas and push her to nursery, relieved that she faces away from me so I don't have to make inane faces or spout gibberish, just to please them. When I return, I slump on the couch and battle with the voices until they convince me that I should eat.

Sometimes, when the voices recede enough to allow me to rest, I can manage a short walk, but this is becoming increasingly unappealing as I don't want to interact with others. I don't want to be bothered with small talk, baby talk or contact of any kind. Nothing appeals, nothing seems worth the energy. I'm getting short-tempered with everyone, especially those near to me, those I move around this box with. When my husband returns from work, I hand over the child and slope off to bed where I can nurse the chaos in my head. I used to feel guilt, so much guilt, but now I know he can do a better job, as he's so keen to remind me every day; 'You might as well crawl back in your pit for all the good you're doing here.'.

What have I become? When you buy a new fairy for the Christmas tree and it's all sparkly and white and everyone looks up at it and sighs, that's how I felt when we met. Now, my hair is matted, my head is on a slant and the magic dust disappeared long ago when I stepped into the fog. I can't blame him for feeling frustrated, angry even. When I fantasised about being a mother, I was sure I could do better job than mine. When my child was stirring inside me, the love I felt was overwhelming. I couldn't wait to show this child all the love I was storing up, couldn't wait to show my baby how much it was wanted, how precious it was. Now, I don't even have the energy or patience to talk to her. I can't seem to shake away this lethargy. I know that history is repeating itself around me, but I'm too tired to stop it.

I need to put my plan into action, the one I decided on when I was 'temporarily out of action', like the song 'Killer Queen', except I'm a killer mum, who slowly smothers the life out of everyone around her, the kind who could snuff your light out just by being there.

I know I need to go, that it's best for everyone, but it's not going to be easy, because I don't have my own money anymore. I'm going to have to withdraw it from the joint account. That should be easy enough, I can do it over a few days until I have enough to see me through for a few weeks. I'll just have to hope that he doesn't check it. Then, I'll need to find somewhere to stay, which is going to be tricky as my friends are all local, so it wouldn't be a good idea to stay with them. As for my family, they're the root of all my problems so I need to make a clean break from them and everything else around here. That means moving away as far as I possibly can, but where to?

I go over to the sideboard and pull out the road atlas, flick through the pages until I come to the South West. That's it! Brighton, a new start in Brighton, maybe things will be brighter in Brighton. I doubt it, but I'm sure they'll be brighter here without me. I'm going to run away and I don't know if I feel scared or excited. What kind of mother runs away? My mother. And me.

I wonder if my mother was mad like me. I wonder if the same thing happened to her. I reason that she was a worse person than me because she left us with him, with a father who was violent. I'm leaving my child with a capable father who works and provides. But am I really any better? What's the alternative? I can't just sit here day after day, wallowing in my own sweat and self-pity, fighting this fight I have every day with myself, with the words in my head. I can't even dress myself, let alone care for this demanding little being that is my child. I can't ruin her life as well as my own, she deserves more than this. She needs to be looked after and cared for and loved. I can do neither. All I can do is mope about the house, getting in everyone's way and causing tension. At least when I'm gone, the arguments will stop and they can have a bit of peace. Things will be better without me souring the milk. Maybe if this cloud ever lifts, I'll come back and things will be different. That's why I didn't decide on the other route. Besides being scared, there's no way back from there. At least now there's a slight chance that my child could have a mother in the future.

It's surprisingly easy to pack up my bags and take

Laura around to her grandma's, where she'll stay until her dad returns from work. Although I'm heading off into the unknown, I feel calm and more in control than I've felt for a long time, the packing of my things serving to reassure me that, soon, this episode in my so-called life will be over. I push the buggy down the driveway, passing brightly-coloured pot plants and manicured hedges. She opens the door, but doesn't greet me, just turns and walks back into the living room. Laura starts to babble and she tries to escape the reigns, so I pop the buckle and she clambers down and toddles into the house. I follow her in and stand in the doorway, slumped against the jamb. Her Grandma's face lights up at the sight of her and she holds out her arms, then lifts her onto her knee. She starts to sing nursery rhymes, clapping hands and laughing, doing the things I should be doing, if I could be bothered. Laura giggles and looks happier that she has done all morning and this both compounds my misery and metaphorically pats my hand; I've done the right thing. I can see the beauty of my child, but I can't feel it. Every moment I spend with her makes me hate myself more. I despise the way I've turned out, hate this mindset I'm trapped in. Why can't I love this little being who brings so much joy to others?

"Why are you crying Alison?" she asks.

"I don't know, I'm just down, that's all."

"I don't know how you find time to be down with this one, she's a bundle of energy, she is. I didn't have time to be down when James was little, I was too busy caring for him."

She looks right through me, her posh little mouth pursing into a cat's arse and I can't wait to get my useless, grubby being out of her sterile house. I hand over the bag and I cannot find any words, so I slope off without speaking.

"What time will you pick her up?" she asks.

"When I'm ready," I say.

I walk back home and collect my bags, which I haul to the bus stop. Today is the day I leave my baby and I'm hating every atom in my miserable body because of it, but I know it's what I need to do.

The train ride is tedious but soothing, giving me a welcome break from the stagnancy of a home I could only glide through and a role which didn't befit me. I sink my head back into the seat and close my eyes. I can feel the quickness of my heart in my chest so I try to breathe deeply, to calm down. I feel like I've been caught stealing, except I've not taken anything, just left it behind. I imagine what they will say when they find out. They'll say that they always knew I was no good, what did they expect of someone like me? He's going to be so angry and she's going to say, 'I told you so.' I hope he's not so angry that he takes it out on Laura. I've done this so she can have a better life.

When I arrive in Brighton, I'm tired, but the need to find accommodation spurs me on and I find Tourist Information nestled between a coffee shop and Mothercare.

"Can I help you?" the lady says in a funny accent.

'I doubt it,' I think. I tell her that I'm looking for a place to stay for a few days, that it needs to be cheap and that it needs to be near the centre. She busies herself looking through files and consulting with her colleague. I imagine the bedlam that's going on at home. His mother's irritation when I didn't come back, his irritation when he found the note. I wonder if he was shocked or relieved.

"The only room I can find is about a mile out of town. It's cheap and cheerful, but I believe it's clean and the lady that runs it is very nice."

"I'll take it."

She hands me a piece of paper with the address and a hastily drawn map of how to find it. I thank her and pull my case out onto the street. I decide to walk the mile, rather than spend money on a taxi. The bags are heavy and awkward, but I reckon I deserve to suffer for what I've done today. I've lied, I've deceived and I've abandoned the child I couldn't wait to welcome into the world.

The guest house is small and basic, but clean. I spend two weeks there in all, resting, thinking, licking my wounds and trying to forget. The last thing I see in my mind's eye, before sleep, is the face of my baby, my daughter, but when I hear myself saying those words, it just feels wrong. It's not true. I don't deserve to think of myself as a mother because I've not really been one for a long time. Not since those first few months when the bond with my new born was strong and safe, before the cloud came. I would hold her and nuzzle my face into her creased little neck which smelled of talcum powder and sweetness. The weight of her tiny body in my arms or over my shoulder felt like nothing I've ever held before. I would reach down and stroke her waxy little feet, whisper into her ear, tell her 'mummy loves you.' She would try to focus her blinking eyes on my face, her head wobbling, me holding it, keeping her safe.

All this thinking about the past, about her, is doing me no good at all and I decide that the only way to survive is to get her out of my head completely. I've come all this way to start afresh, to recover and that means I need to lock away the secrets of my past.

CHAPTER 11

Snippets of a New Life
1985 - 1994

It's been six weeks since I moved down here and, thanks to the owner of the Guest House, a lovely lady called Marjorie, I now have a 'little job' at the local pub. My funds are running low, so I'm glad of the work, but I need to find something to supplement this income so that I can afford to rent somewhere on a more permanent basis. I'm renting a tiny box room, for now, in the home of one of Marjorie's friends. It's cheaper than the guest house, but I feel like I have to watch my every move and that's what I've tried to get away from. So far though, I'm happy with the way things have turned out. I've formed a bond, of sorts, with Marjorie, although our friendship is all based on lies. She thinks I've had my heart broken by a failed love affair, which isn't that far from the truth. That explains my fluctuating moods and the tears, my desire to be alone.

I'm beginning to feel better about life now, maybe because I'm not responsible for anyone else, not responsible for hurting anyone. The job at the pub has given me a purpose and I enjoy serving people from different walks of life. The thing is, they know nothing about me and I can pretend that I'm a carefree twenty-something, enjoying life in a different town. Serving beer and passing the day with small talk suits me just fine, there's no need to disclose anything at all, where I've come from or who I really am. Their questions about my past are met with a coy smile and flippant comments, 'that's for me to know.' My confidence has soared because I'm doing something I can do well, not failing as I did before. This is the best and worst thing I could have done, but I'm focussing on the positive, so that I can move on.

After a couple of years of working behind the bar, supplemented by shop work, a chance meeting and a flippant comment leads me along another path. I'm on the bus back to bedsit land and another evening cooped up with only my books for company. I spot a lady paying her fare. She's carrying a brief case and a hessian bag loaded with books. She plonks herself next to me, trapping my skirt under her leg. I tug it out and shuffle closer to the window, unable to see the outside world through the fog of condensation.

"Sorry about that," she says, "it's a bit murky out there isn't it?"

"Yeah, I can't see a thing," I reply.

She settles down into her seat and takes a book out, opening it and squinting to find the place she wants. I notice the title.

"The Colour Purple," I say, "I read that once, a while ago."

"Did you? What did you think of it?"

"I couldn't believe the injustice. It was sad how these people were trapped in this life they had no control over.

It wasn't even that long ago either," I replied, feeling the urge to stop there, before I went on too much.

"Did you study it at 'A' Level?"

"No, I didn't do 'A' Levels," I reply, feeling inferior again.

"Really? You seem like an intelligent girl," she says, smiling at me, almost pityingly.

"Hardly a girl," I reply.

"Well, compared to me."

"I wish I was a girl, wish I could do the girl thing all over again," I say, then wish I hadn't.

"Don't we all," she says wistfully.

A silence follows and I pretend to look out of the misty window but she knows I can't see. What she says next surprises me.

"I was a bit of a sad case, when I was a girl, had a rough start in life, you could say."

I look at her expensive brief case, her glossy hair, perfect make up and designer boots.

"You don't look like much of a sad case now," I say.

I wonder why I'm speaking so openly to someone I've never met. Maybe I feel a connection, maybe she has a trusting face.

"Something someone once said to me changed my life," she said.

"Pray tell."

"They said 'Never let your past determine your future' and I never understood it."

"I can see why. I mean, however much we try to hide from a past, it still makes us what we are," I answer.

"That's exactly what I used to think until that comment made me flip it on its head," she said.

"So, what did you do?" I asked, feeling confident enough to question the life of a stranger.

"I decided that I wasn't going to be that lost little girl any more. The very next day, I booked some counselling sessions and an assertiveness course! I've never looked back. It was the kick up the arse I needed. Sorry for swearing."

The conversation continues in the same vein, until it's my stop. I reluctantly stand, not wanting to leave this fascinating lady with the story of hope.

"It was great to meet you Dawn. You've certainly given me food for thought."

"Great to meet you too. Now go get 'em girl!" she says.

When I get home, I search my cupboards for a book I was given a long time ago, a kind of self-help manual which I dismissed as rubbish. Dawn's story has struck a chord and I have the beginnings of a fire in the pit of my stomach, one which I want to feed and exploit. By the time I've finished the first couple of chapters, it's midnight and I'm grinning, revelling in thoughts of making my life count.

Next time I finish my morning shift at the shop, I take the bus up to the university campus and I seek out information on courses. It seems that I have sufficient 'O' levels, but I would have to take a couple of 'A' levels at night school. I make the decision; I would take English and Sociology as soon as I possibly could, after all, my evenings often stretched out before me if I wasn't working, so this would be a sensible way of spending them. Who knows where it would lead?

Surprisingly, I find both courses interesting and quite easy to get through. I come out with and 'A' for English and 'B' for Sociology, which opens the door to a few options, but I settle on Law.

Law is not the easiest subject to study, but I'm grateful that I have finally been accepted on to the course. Life is a lot better for me now, at least emotionally. I find that I can talk to people quite easily, instead of shying away from conversations. I join debates and speak passionately on subjects which ignite a spark. My previous life is becoming more and more of a distant memory, the image of my child fading as fast as the memories I hold. I have started to believe that I really am this person I'm merely portraying.

While some of my younger peers enjoy the full university life of drinking and sleeping around, I prefer to dip in and out as it suits. Most days I go back home to study, living close enough to campus to do so. On the odd occasion that I do join in the fun, I always make sure I keep control of my senses, afraid of giving away the person I am underneath. I don't want any of them to know about her.

I have concocted a story about my past. I was put in a care home at a young age and had never wanted to find my parents. Most people don't probe and, if they do, I make sure I change the subject.

University life suits me well. When I look back at the person who ran away, I hardly recognise her. It worries me that I have done such a good job of hiding her, but I know it has been necessary to my healing. Whenever I start to doubt myself, I think of Dawn and her words; 'Don't let your past shape your future.'

I come out of Uni with a 2:1 and a confidence I thought I could never wear. I have many mantras, which I repeat whenever the seeds of self-doubt try to root in my mind. My mantras help me through, reassure me that the I deserve this new life, that I belong here. The stranger I was years ago is disappearing with every new avenue I explore.

I start my career at a small back-street firm, learning the rudiments in my chosen field of family law. It's a tough world and it takes an abundance of tenacity and will-power to survive the first two years. Eventually, I move up to a bigger firm which specialises in personal injury, which is where the next part of my life starts.

CHAPTER 12

Harry
1994

That day I strode into the office and plonked myself in the chair opposite Alison.

"You're a mystery to me, so you are, Miss Alison," I said, trying to hide my nerves with a smile.

"Really? Good," She replied, not looking up from the file she was buried in.

"A true mystery. I know this sounds corny, but I've been pondering why someone as attractive as you, doesn't have a partner, a husband even."

"You work in law and you think it's a mystery? It's like working in a school then deciding not to have kids," she said.

"Smart as well. I really don't know how you've slipped through the net."

"I've never swam anywhere near the net."

"See? You're witty, you're charming and beautiful to boot. How about making an old man very happy by agreeing to come for drinks after work?"

Drinks after work lead to dinner, theatre visits, pub lunches and, before you know it, we were in a relationship. We were both busy with our lives, especially with the work load, but Alison fascinated me enough to want a long-lasting commitment. It's true, she was a bit 'closed', there were swathes of her life which remained a mystery and she always changed the subject when I tried to get more of an insight into her childhood years, but this made her even more beguiling and attractive to me. There was a deep sadness behind those beautiful eyes of hers.

We saw each other for about a year before I asked her to move in with me, 'You can't spend the rest of your life in bedsit land,' I told her. She said she needed to think very carefully about it and the shutters came down, but after about a week, she agreed and we moved her belongings into my place. I was surprised and saddened by how little she had accumulated for someone in their thirties. She shrugged it off, said she was never one for material things. That made sense. She was never one to want labels on her clothes or bags, but she always looked classy and smart.

We settled into an easy kind of life together, making the most of weekends when the constraints of the office lifted a little and we could relax on long walks or lazy Sunday lunches in country pubs. After a year, we decided to get married. It wasn't the romantic proposal conveyed in TV dramas or books, but a practical decision, based on the 'next step' towards joint property ownership. You would think that this would be the prompt to 'come clean' about her past, but she didn't, so I stopped asking. We invited a few mutual friends and my family to a simple registry office ceremony, followed by a meal. I tried not to harp on about how sorry I felt for her not having any family to share our special day, 'are you sure you don't want a big white wedding, I thought it was every girl's dream?' She muttered something about not being that kind of girl and I accepted it.

We settled into a routine of work, meals out and weekend walks. The inevitable discussions about having children came and went, she explained that her reluctance to start a family was because she couldn't give them the attention they deserve, having such a busy job. I said that I understood, but I had always wanted children, and never more so than when I met Alison. She would have made a great mother. I didn't give up without a fight. I engineered pub lunches with friends who had the most adorable kids, hoping it would prompt her instinct, kick start her motherly hormones or something. Eventually, she snapped and told me that I had to stop. It was never mentioned again, but for me, it was always there and things started to deteriorate.

I know that I stopped being so caring and considerate. I never spoke of my resentment, but it was slowly eating away at me. Every time we passed a pram or a toddler, my heart would sink and I'd torture myself by peering inside at the tiny bundle or the rosy-cheeked toddler. 'I want that,' I would think. I stayed at the office later and later, citing the increasing work load, but I think she knew it was because she was denying me access to the world of 'family'. I said that I understood her reasons, but I didn't. I thought everything would fall into place if we gave it our best shot. She had an answer for everything, 'You can't 'just give it a try,' she would say, 'we're talking about little beings whose lives we would be fully responsible for. They don't come 'on approval',

you can't send them back if you're not totally satisfied.'
Then she would break down and go and lie down. I
would hear her crying, but she didn't want me near her.
She shut down and shut me out.

We carried on, trying to convince ourselves that we
had a decent life, while all the time skirting around
each other, like we were in a kind of 'waggle dance';
'Waggle dance; a figure of eight movement that worker
bees perform to indicate the location of a food source',
except we were just avoiding each other, moving around
our home in circles, deftly avoiding contact and the truth.

Eventually, our relationship broke down. It hurt a lot,
but I regret to say, I never really showed with words or
actions, how much it destroyed me to see the beautiful
woman I fell in love with slip through my fingers.

CHAPTER 13

The Reunion
2012

When the case hit my desk, all I wanted to do was escape. I escaped in drink for a while, but that didn't help anyone. Then I buried myself in work to minimise the time spent at home. Life with Harry has become unbearable. I can't look him in the eye. I married him under false pretences and soon he will know what a fake I am, but that doesn't matter for now. I've decided that I can't run any longer. I need to face this 'problem' head-on, as I would advise others to do in this situation. My sister is dying. My sister who brought me up as her own when she was only sixteen! How could I have been so heartless? How could I have left them all behind? That doesn't matter now either. Funny how death overrides everything else. There's a chance I might have this disease too, but that's another problem for another day. I've got to take this one step at a time.

Today is the day I face up to my demons, meet up with the past which has been buried under layers of lies. Today is the day when reality drags me kicking and screaming from my bubble of pretence.

I check the number on the door and walk up the path not knowing if I want to knock or not. I have arrived at the home of Sylvia and her husband, Paul. My sister Sylvia who tended to my needs as a child, who dressed me, fed me and cared for me and who I so heartlessly dumped, along with all the others. My nerves are in shreds and I need to take back some control of the feelings which run rampant and threaten to undo me. I try to focus on my breathing, but I can't push away the fear. There's so much at stake. This meeting could be a huge determiner on how well I cope with the next chapter. If my sister judges me for what I did, then I don't know how this would affect me, how I would cope with the negative impact. I've not even plucked up the courage to tell my husband the whole truth of what went before, not explained where I am today. What good would it do anyway? He 'doesn't do drama.' But even though our relationship has deteriorated to the point where we hardly have a relationship at all, I still want his approval.

A shadow appears at the glass and the door opens. I assume it's Paul and I offer my hand out to him, hoping he doesn't ignore it. To my relief, he takes it gently in his and beckons for me to come in.

"You have to be Alison, you have the same eyes," he says.

His warmth goes some way to easing my anxiety, but still I fuss with my coat and scarf, avoiding eye contact, delaying the need for small talk, the inevitable questions. Paul offers to take my things and, as I hand them to him, I catch sight of a figure in the living room. She's almost swamped by the cushions which surround her in the armchair, but I can see the family likeness; our family likeness. She doesn't get up to greet me, but she does manage a smile. She looks thin, frail and wan. I want to turn and run away from the shame that hits me as I register just how sick she is. She starts to cry and I walk over and hug her gently.

"Alright our kid?" I manage, amazed with the ease at which I slip back to my Northern roots.

Any fool can see that she isn't alright, that her cheeks are sunken and she's thin, so thin. I slide on to the arm of the chair and take her tiny hand in mine, not letting her frail fingers escape.

"I'm so glad you came, so glad I got to see you again. I've missed you, we all have. We had no idea you were planning to leave, no idea at all."

"I'm sorry," I say, but it hardly seems enough for a lifetime of desertion.

"We just didn't understand why you went without saying anything. We knew you were down, but we didn't expect you to leave, honestly we didn't."

"It wasn't me, really. Wasn't me who walked out that day, it was someone else. That's the only way I can explain it."

"Well I'm glad you came back, whoever you are."

We laugh then and the years of absence melt away. She talks about the family she has made, nods to the pictures of her children, three beaming faces smiling for the camera, her and Paul behind, proud and parental. I tell her about my recovery in Brighton and how I could never find a way back. She reassures me that it doesn't matter, that the important thing is that I'm back now so that she could see me again, so that she could know I'm alright.

"When James found out you'd gone, he was fuming."

"I bet he was."

"He didn't know where you could have gone, how you could have left Laura. I must admit, I found that hard as well, especially having kids of my own."

"Like I said, Sylvia, I was someone else then. I was a kid and I didn't understand myself what was happening to me, how could I expect anyone else to?"

"I know. We were all young when we had kids, still kids ourselves weren't we?"

"We were, but it looks like you've made a better job of it than I did. I honestly thought that everyone would be better off without me. I realise now that I was ill, but at the time I thought I was mad, and maybe I was."

"I've told you it doesn't matter. It's a wonder any of us have turned out 'normal' after what we went through anyway."

Those words were like a soothing salve on an open sore. I had always thought it was no use blaming your upbringing for all your shortcomings, but now I realise that you can't escape it. Like a bee sting, you need to tease it out so it can stop hurting you.

"Now, don't get upset when I say this but I've not got long, Alison. I'm dying our kid and there's nothing anyone can do."

She slumps further into the chair and there isn't anything as important as this moment, this reconnection with a past I so naively thought I could forget.

"I'm so sorry for running away, for not being there. I don't expect you to understand, don't expect anyone to, it's just what I had to do."

Sylvia lifts her head and looks at me directly. I can't

fathom whether it's pain in her eyes or just plain sorrow, but she looks completely broken.

"It's the kids, she whispers, "I can't cope with not being there for them."

My heart breaks for her and withers with the guilt at what I have done. At least I had the chance to be around for mine, but I chose not to. Paul comes back into the room carrying two cups and a look of concern.

"Come on love, try not to get too upset."

I take one of the cups from him, mouthing 'I'm sorry' as I do so. Paul slides onto the arm of the chair and there's an awkward silence waiting to be filled, but nobody can find the right words. What do you say to someone you hardly know and to a sister who is losing her fight for life?

"I don't know what to say Sylvia, I can't begin to imagine how you feel."

"I hope you never know how I feel, which reminds me, you need to get the test Alison, you all do. I thought I had IBS, thought I'd be all right if I just managed my diet, but nothing changed, then I found out I had this. It's her you know, me mam, she's passed it on. The only thing she's ever given me!"

An involuntary laugh escapes my lips. "I'm so sorry Sylvia, it's not funny, but that's exactly what I thought as soon as I heard the news. The only thing she could give us is a sodding disease."

Sylvia's eyes crinkle and she squeezes my hand. It was as if all those years dissolved and we'd never lost touch.

"I'm so glad I came today Sylvia, I mean that with all my heart."

She squeezes my hand again and promptly falls asleep.

While she sleeps, Paul keeps himself busy making tea and filling me in on the many years of their lives that I've missed. We look at family photographs and I feel more than grateful that he finds me worthy enough to share them. A thousand thoughts flit through my mind. I have been in denial all these years and for all these years, lives have carried on, family history has been made and people have made a mark on this Earth for themselves and their children. What have I done? I have hidden myself away and become a false non-being, living a false non-life. Looking through these pictures brings home to me just how stupid and naïve I've been to think that running away was the best thing I could do. I can see with great clarity now that it was probably the worst thing. It makes me realise just how warped my mind must have been to think I could escape my past. I could have been the one in these pictures with my child, or children if I'd have gone on to have more. It could have been me making history and making a mark in the world. Instead I scuttled away and hid, made another 'life' for myself, lived a charade for all this time and now I know what it's like to regret something.

I look at my sister sleeping in the chair. She is small and lost, just like a child. It takes me back to when we were all small and lost, to when we needed to be rescued but it never happened. I think of the irony of life, how someone like Sylvia, who has battled against all odds to make a stable family life, is now having it all taken away from her. Where is the justice in that? It should be me! It's me who deserves this fate, not my sister who always looked after us, then went on to have a family of her own, not our Sylvia who deserves so much more. I cry for what could have been, for how our lives could have been different had we found each other sooner, had I not been so consumed with the idea of disappearing. What if I'd stuck it out and got better, made a good wife and mother?

Then I remind myself that life is full of 'what ifs'. I couldn't imagine life being good for my daughter if I'd have stayed. I couldn't imagine ever getting better if I hadn't taken myself away. I can only wonder how much longer it would have been before the madness completely took me. What would life have been like then? I snap back to reality and look up at Paul. He's crying quietly and I put my arm around him so that we form a human cradle around Sylvia.

"She's been such a good mum," he says.

"She always was," I reply.

"I wish I could have been. A good mum," I say, but it sounds self-indulgent and I'm here to see Sylvia, not to analyse my own failings.

"Sylvia told me a bit about why you went away, how you were ill."

"At the time, I didn't think I was ill, I thought I was incapable, not cut out for it, thought I would go under if I stayed any longer."

"Yeah well, times change and we know a lot more about it now, don't we?"

"Do we?" I ask.

Paul clears away the cups, then we talk about the kids, about his plans for them and I'm overcome by a heavy sadness. She desperately wants to stay with her kids and she can't, I desperately wanted to leave. For the first time, I feel something different. Instead of feeling guilt, I feel an enormous sense of injustice. What happened to me was out of my control, I just didn't know at the time. Things could have been very different if only I knew that what was happening to me, if only I knew it wasn't something I willed on myself.

Back home, I sit in a dazed state and let the thoughts take over. Reuniting with my sister has caused no end of memory flashes and I feel mentally vulnerable, afraid that the episode during my twenties is going to be repeated, so I'm resting for a few days at home. I'm not sure if I'm doing the right thing of not, because I've been overcome by a stultifying lethargy and I can't seem to get going with anything. Tasks, like washing a few pots, which would normally take five minutes, are being strung out over hours while an internal debate is playing in my head around whether or not I can muster the energy to move. Changing the bed yesterday completely wiped me out and I crawled into it and slept for hours. Then there is the relentless vice that grips my head and squeezes with no sign of mercy so that I feel my skull could burst at any moment and spill its contents. When the thoughts and the voices from the past subside, they are replaced by the song on a loop, an incessant repetition of a melody and words which evoke fear but I don't know why, 'this could be the last time, this could be the last time, maybe the last time, I don't know'. I decide to go the doctor sooner, rather than later, because, this time, I know the warning signs and I want to be in control, to stop this in its tracks so it doesn't get a hold on me like it did when I was younger.

The doctor looks up at me over his glasses and asks what he can do for me. Déjà vu.

"It's a long story, I don't know where to start really, but I feel awful, like there's a vice gripping my head and a constant song on a loop going around and around." I look at him, waiting for him to ask those inane questions but he doesn't, he just waits. I shift in my chair and bow my head. I want to go home but I know that I need to sit this out.

"I had a breakdown in my twenties and I'm scared I'm going there again. I can't seem to do anything without a massive effort and I feel like my head will explode. I've tried painkillers, hot baths, watching crap TV, sorry for swearing, but nothing works. I feel like I can't escape from my own head!"

"How long have you felt like this?"

"For a while, but especially since I met my sister recently. It just triggered memories of the past, who I was before. It made me realise why I ran away in the first place, but I had no choice really but to meet her, she's terminally ill, you see and she had information for me."

"Right……"

"She has bowel cancer, the only thing our dear mother ever gave her. Sweet Christ. She looks awful, all thin and grey and wasted like those beautiful lilies that flop over the vase when they're spent, all the life sucked out of them, from beauty to floppy grey mess."

I stop talking, aware that I'm losing my composure,

losing focus. I don't want the doctor to think I'm a bumbling, irrational mess.

"You say she has hereditary bowel cancer?"

"Yes, she's been told that, yes."

"How old is your sister?"

"She's fifty-eight, but she won't see fifty-nine, or even the next month."

"I'm so sorry to hear that. Look, the priority here is to get you tested, keep you monitored and to address your other health issues. I can start by taking a sample today, the receptionist will sort you out with the necessary kit. Regarding your present state of mind, we have a couple of options, long-term, but I think, for now, you would benefit from some mild tranquilisers to get you through this trauma."

I nod and fall into myself. I don't want any of this, but I know what happened last time, when I rebelled against the pills, so I take the prescription and the test kit and I go home, curl up like a hedgehog and weep. So many tears. I don't know how long I lie there, but, when my husband arrives home from work, he looks visibly shocked.

"Bloody hell Alison, are you still crying? You look shocking. Don't you think you should stop this now, you need to think about going to work, getting back to normal."

"Normal? Tell me what normal is and I'll get back to it."

"Oh, very funny. There's no helping you is there? You're always the victim, aren't you? Never want anyone to comment or help. I might as well not be here."

I look at him in disbelief, not understanding how the man I married could be so cold and out of touch. He goes upstairs, flashing me a scowl of hatred which worsens the vice around my head. I reach for the tablets, hardly able to control the shaking, but manage to pop one out of its bubble and swallow it. I can hear banging and mumbling upstairs but can't muster a response to it, or anything else.

When I wake up, my neck hurts and my head feels thick, but not vice-ridden. My throat is parched, I could drink a reservoir, but when I try to stand, my legs wobble and it takes three attempts. I stumble to the kitchen like someone twice my age and, on automatic pilot, fill the kettle and switch it on. I listen at the bottom of the stairs for noises above, but there's only silence and I'm relieved that I don't have to deal with any more confrontations. I go in to the bathroom and see the plastic pot and spatula taunting me from the shelf. 'Oh yes, I know you're there, I'd forgotten about you for a minute, but I know you're there. I'll deal with you later.' My body is doing things it hasn't done for a while and it frightens me. There's a heaviness in my chest, a weakness in my arms and a wobble in my legs, but I'm not going to let it beat me this time.

I reach for the medication and read the instructions, 'one to be taken four times a day'. I cannot quite work it out through my mental fog, but I think it might be too soon for another one just yet. 'Not to be taken with alcohol'. I can't even be bothered with getting dressed, never mind putting my face on to go out and, fortunately, I've never been one to drink in the house, especially alone. For a second I wonder where you are, where you've gone, but then I decide that I'm not going to waste time fretting about it, so I go back to making the tea. I pour the scalding water on top of the bag and frighten myself with thoughts of pouring it over myself, so I hastily put the kettle back on its stand. I take every one of the kitchen knives off the metal strip on the wall and hide them in the drawer, my hands shaking. I stand for a moment, hunched over the worktop, the cold of the granite reminding me I can feel.

Sometime later I hear you huffing and puffing next to me in the bed, pulling at the quilt, throwing your body around. I get up and wordlessly relocate to the spare room. I have no energy to deal with this now, can't think with a head as thick as concrete. I just want to hide and sleep. You shout through the wall, "that's right, just walk away." I think 'I will, I will walk away,' but then I think 'that's what she would do, what I did before, and I don't want to be that person.'

In the waiting room, a few days later, I choose a seat in the corner and sit with my head down. With plenty of empty seats around me, I'm less likely to get some inane person rattling on about the shortcomings of the NHS. I take out my Kindle so that I can check my emails, then think better of it and tuck it away. I avoid eye-contact with the others, not wanting to engage in any way, not wanting them to intrude on my sphere of safety. I can't be bothered with talking, it uses up too much energy, so I sit and look down into my own sorry lap. Finally, my name is called, but I'm so lost in my thoughts that it takes a few seconds to register and when I do, I jerk and curse, like someone with Tourette's and my phone drops to the floor. The cover pings off and flies under the chair of the lady opposite, the battery lands under my own seat. I can feel the tears at the corner of my eyes, the lack of control, the feeling that all eyes are upon me and I get up slowly, side-stepping the disassembled phone and it reminds me of me. The battery is my brain which has taken temporary residence somewhere else. I get down on hands on knees to gather each piece of the dismembered phone and the lady passes me the cover and a look of pity. It takes all my willpower not to snatch it from her and mutter expletives. Does she not know that I'm a fucking Lawyer, that I'm perfectly fucking competent? I don't need her pity or anyone else's. She's still looking at me with that droopy sad face and I could knock it back to normality if I was that way inclined. When I try to put my phone back together my hands are shaking so much, that it's the best I can do to bungle it into my bag, still in bits. The young nurse beckons me to follow her and she skips ahead of me, but I shuffle slowly behind like Mary's errant lamb. She pushes open the door and the consultant, all grey hair, glasses and pompous bloody manner, looks up from my file and I want to turn and walk the other way, but I know that would be stupid.

"Come in, take a seat. How have you been feeling?"

"I've felt better."

I hate this non-person I've become, always down and depressed.

"I'm normally as sharp as a tack you know," I say, trying to convince the doctor that what he sees is a false representation of me.

"You've had a lot on your mind, I'm sure. Now, we do have the results of your test back and it does show some blood so, given the family history, we need to undertake further investigations so that we can get a clearer picture."

"Right. So, what does that mean? Does that mean I've got the same as my sister?"

"I'm sure you'll understand that it's impossible to say at this stage. It can be present for all sorts of reasons which we need to rule out. The next step is to do a CT colonography, which will give us a clearer idea of what we're dealing with. We'll book you in for that and you should get your appointment in the next couple of weeks."

I stand up and say my thanks, glad to leave so that I can scurry home and be alone to nurse my thoughts. I have two invaders to deal with; the person I was in the past who is infiltrating my mind, thought-by-thought and this disease which threatens to invade my body, cell-by-miserable-cell.

I thought I could escape, forge a new life and bury who I was. I thought I could re-invent myself as a success, carry on through life being admired, people looking up to me, coming to me for advice, respecting me. I got away with it for a while. People bought into my act, believed I was confident, secure and knowledgeable, while all the while I was hiding the truth. They have all been taken in by lies, by the veneer, the façade that hid the monster beneath. The last few months have seen that monster being slowly revealed, coming out from beneath its blanket to take residence in my befuddled mind. I hate this thing I have become again, this ghost, this spirit who floats through the lives of everyone around, leaving poison in its trail. This thing that cannot call itself a mother.

After what has seemed like an endless wait, I'm here again, in the same chair, the same place, awaiting the news that will guide the next chapter. I'm perversely hoping for the worse possible result, so that I can slip away and it won't be my own fault. I'm here alone, my 'other half' has given up on me. He's leaving me to it, doesn't know what to do, can't do right for doing wrong. My solitude is heightened by the presence of couples who are holding hands, chatting, speculating and no doubt offering reassurances. I'm trying to read one of the hospital magazines as a distraction, but I can't focus so I slip it back on the pile. I look ahead and a cheerful presenter flashes his beaming smile at me from the miniature screen, but this only serves to highlight my misery. 'What is wrong with you?' I ask myself, 'you're normally so positive.'

"Alison Benson," calls the nurse and I rise once again to follow her like a little lap dog into the sterile office where my future will be relayed to me.

"Sit down Mrs Benson," the Consultant says and his nurse sits beside him.

I can guess that the news is not good.

"We have the results of your tests and investigations and I'm afraid to say that they do suggest an invasive tumour."

The nurse relocates to the seat next to mine. I don't want her to sit on the seat next to mine and I don't want to be looked at like that. I frown at her and she edges away from me slightly, then I turn my frown on the Consultant. He looks at me impassively, obviously waiting for my reaction, but I feel numb and don't know how to react, so I continue to frown.

"This must be very difficult for you," he says.

I continue to frown at him, as if he is personally

responsible for the results. I imagine a metaphorical tumbleweed passing between us, an indication that the silence has gone on too long, but all I can do is stare at him. I know my stare is hostile but I cannot snap out of it and I don't know what to say. I think of the film 'Sliding Doors' and wished that I had taken the other door, the one that lead somewhere else. The consultant leans back in his chair and I instinctively do the same. We're having a lean-off and a stare-off and I don't know who's winning and I don't care.

"This must be hard for you to take in, Mrs Benson," he says.

The tumbleweed floats off and I sit up.

"What happens next?" I ask, finally finding the words, "when you say invasive, what does that mean? Does it mean that it's spread, that it's spreading right at this very minute?"

"When a tumour is invasive, it has started to infiltrate the surrounding tissue. We would have to do further investigations to get a clearer picture, then we can suggest a treatment plan."

"A treatment plan?" I sit there, reminded of the last time I was offered a treatment plan and I refused. What if I refused again? "What if I refuse a treatment plan?" I spit out the words and the doctor looks suitably affronted.

"Treatments do vary between individuals. Let's see what the scan reveals and take it from there."

"Shit," is all I can muster as a response, then I hang my head and try to compute what has been said.

The nurse takes my hand and I let her.

"We'll put it all in a letter and we'll send you details

of your next appointment, so please don't worry if you can't remember what's been said today. Is there anyone with you?"

"No, but I'm fine," I say, then stand up to leave.

"I'm so sorry, Mrs Benson," the Consultant says.

"It's not your fault," I reply.

Despite my new regime of medication, 'happy pills', my mood does not lift over the next few days. I can see the path of imminent death stretching before me and, suddenly, what I thought I wanted, isn't what I want at all. However, I have no choice but to go with it. Thoughts of my new future invade all others and I'm forced to think about things like surgery, illness and death. Now I'm faced with the final chapter, I'm wondering if I should crawl out of this misery and arrange to see my child, the one I abandoned when I thought it was best. I don't care about anything else, I have no regrets about what I could have been, I just want to see that she's alright, that she's done alright without me. It's not as if I haven't thought about a reunion before, it's been the voice of my conscience since the day I left. I have always come to the same conclusion, that she doesn't need me pushing my nose back into her life, confusing her and those around her. She would never understand how any mother could leave her own child and run away.

I leave the hospital and walk towards the car park, but I feel dizzy, so I sit down on a low wall, try to breathe through it. I stretch out my legs and notice that my tights are laddered, there are splodges of dried-up tea on my shoes and my skirt is creased. I swallow any pride I may have left and phone Harry to see if he could pick me up, because I don't trust myself enough to drive home.

"Is it bad news?" he asks.

"Yes," I say and he agrees to jump in a cab, so that he can drive my car home.

When he arrives and we're both in the car, I tell him about the tumour. His response is not to hug me or reassure me that everything will be alright. He asks one question,

"What about my trip?"

"It's your call," I reply, "it wasn't the first thing that came into my mind, your sojourn to the Alps, so I haven't thought about what will happen with your trip. I have bowel cancer."

"God, I know, I can't believe it."

He turns on the engine and, without another look my way, he drives us home. When we arrive, we don't quite know what to do. I have an urge to tell everyone my news, like it's a piece of gossip that I can't keep to myself. I message a colleague, 'it's cancer,' then I take myself away into the spare room and sit in the dark for a while. It's strange not having a partner to reach out to at a time like this. I thought that, by getting married again, I could create a new family, of sorts, but that wasn't to be. I drift off wondering if I could have been wiser in my choice of husbands. When I awake, he is perched on my bed with a cup of tea.

"I thought you'd like a brew."

"Yeah, thanks, I'm parched."

"So, what happens next, will you'll be going in for surgery soon?"

"I suppose so."

"Have they given you a recovery time?"

"No, they haven't. It's a major op and I'm guessing everyone is different, but from what I can glean, I could be off work for six months or more."

"We'll struggle if it's more."

"What do you mean?"

"I mean, you get paid for six months, but after that we'll struggle."

"What will be will be. I might not even be here in six months' time. Have you thought of that one? I haven't really thought about the money aspect, I'm still grappling with the disease."

"I know, so am I, but we have to be practical."

"Well how about planning my funeral then, that would be practical wouldn't it?"

He leaves the room and I wonder if he knows how much his cold practicality hurts. I find it quite odd that someone could be so lacking in compassion and empathy. Then I realise that it was cold practicality that made me leave my child. Lack of compassion and empathy? Tick that box too. My child must have felt a hurt a million times more powerful than this when she grew up and realised that her own mother had deserted her. I need her to know how much I regret that day.

As promised, further tests take place and a treatment plan is suggested. Cutting through the jargon, one thing stands out, I'll need a colostomy bag. Although this is no time to be vain, I imagine it bulging beneath the once-smooth lines of a pencil skirt or leaking out to sully the white silk of an otherwise pristine shirt, a brown-green splurge spreading and stinking, invading my perfection, just like the cancer.

The date for surgery plops through the letterbox one dull day in October. I pick up the brown envelope and, as I do, I'm distracted by something moving in the garden. It's a single magpie hopping around the lawn, a portent of bad luck and the thief of happiness. The letter informs me that a bed has been booked in three weeks' time, three weeks of waiting, which I will spend at home trying to redesign my future

In the following days and weeks, I deal with a few phone calls about important cases, but most of my time is spent trying to relax and escape the maudlin thoughts. Harry skirts around me, not knowing what to do. He isn't coming forward with affection or kind words and, although we've grown apart over the last couple of years, I did hope that something as serious as this could change us into being more 'together'. I know that I've not been very nice to him either, but I thought he could see past this, see the fear. It hurts, but I'm too proud to tell him that all I need is to be someone's 'someone special', especially at a time like this. I've done a lot of thinking during my time at home and I've come to the sad conclusion that I never was his 'someone special', that he was always a bit of a loner and things were always destined to be this way. I knew this, but I chose to marry him anyway, so I am equally to blame for the breakdown. There's nothing quite like cancer to make you acutely aware of the shortcomings in your life and to emphasise how lonely you really are.

The agonising wait is over, the day of surgery has arrived. In his wisdom, Harry has decided not to have time off work as my surgery is not until tomorrow and he might as well wait until then before he books a day off. Sad thing is, I know his boss and she would undoubtedly let him take as much time as he wants, given the circumstances. He swings his car up to the main entrance, keeps the engine running, his hand on the gear stick. I reach for my handbag and remind him not to drive off before I've got my other bag out of the boot. If he can't be arsed with emotional partings, then neither can I, so I mumble a quick 'see you later' and go to the boot to get my bag out.

"Who are the chocolates for? And the pink fizz?" I ask.

"What chocolates?"

"The ones in your boot with the pink fizz."

"Oh, they're for Charlotte at work, it's a big birthday."

"Bloody charming," I reply and walk off muttering about big bloody birthdays and big bloody operation days.

He doesn't offer to carry my bag or help me to find the ward, doesn't even grace me with a backward look, just drives away. I follow the sign to the ward and show my letter to the staff on the front desk.

"Do you have someone with you love?"

"No, not in mind, nor in body, it seems."

"Sorry?"

"I'm not down for surgery until tomorrow, he's gone to work."

They look at each other, then back at me.

"We'll take you into the waiting room, it's going to be

a little while before your bed's ready. There's a snack bar down the corridor if you get peckish and just shout if you need anything else."

I settle into a chair in the corner and mindlessly pick up a magazine, which I flick through, not really taking anything in, just looking at the pictures as a small child would do. I check my phone for the elusive 'I'm so sorry, how thoughtless of me' message but it remains elusive. For a couple of hours, I sit on my perch watching people come and go. Most people have someone with them; a spouse, a mother or a friend. They all wear the same expression of concern. I feel like that tatty Christmas tree fairy again. I reprimand myself for being so self-pitying, but then continue with the thoughts, 'what is so bad about me that I'm here alone without a soul to comfort me?' 'who really cares about me?' and 'what if I die, who would miss me?'

"Mrs Benson?"

I nearly jump out of my skin, so engrossed was I in my misery. I knock the magazine off my knee, which knocks a tea cup off the side. I pull a tissue out to clean up the mess, crouching down on the ground, trying to balance on my haunches but failing miserably. I tipple over and my foot twists beneath me. I fall onto my elbow which gives way.

"Shit," I say.

Everyone in the waiting room is looking at me in disbelief and I feel like shouting 'I'm a fucking solicitor, you know!' but I don't, I just sit there nursing my elbow and crying like a baby.

The nurse takes my arm and tries to pull me up like

you would a toddler who's just thrown a tantrum. The only way I can rise is to kneel up on all fours, my fat arse sticking out, resplendent for all to see. With the help of the nurse, I manage to regain my composure, at least physically. She takes the big bag and I throw my handbag over my shoulder. Tepid tea drips on to my skirt and trickles down my leg.

"Let's get you to the ward, shall we?"

I'm led away, shuffling along like a confused elderly person. All I need now is a pair of tartan slippers with pompoms. I laugh and the nurse smiles down at me. I shuffle along, giggling and crying at the same time, feeling like I've lost it completely, but not really caring. I just want to get in that bed, get that scratchy, starchy gown on, pull the sheets up and wallow in my own miserable tears.

I would say that I've never felt so isolated, but that wouldn't be true. Even during my marriages, I have felt like a solitary tourist. I have never understood how that can be, how you can live in the same house as someone, but feel lonelier and more cut off than ever. This disease seems to have given me the ability to see things clearly. If I've only got a short time left, why spend it with someone I don't love and who doesn't even care about me, let alone love me? I decide that I need to break away so that I can find peace before I die. I know in my heart that the only way to do this is to fully reconnect with my past, with that child who grew in my womb, who lit up my world when I saw her beautiful, perfect little face with the rosebud lips, the little downy cheeks and the blonde crown of wispy hair. The child I brought into this world with the waxy feet and the weight of her tiny body nestled in my arm. I ache to have that moment again, to be given that chance to be a mother, a mother who deserves the title, instead of the one I became.

After a fretful night, I am awoken by the moans of the lady in the opposite bed, who is clearly in pain. The nurse goes to her assistance, sitting her up and handing her some tablets. She guides the cup to her mouth so she can swallow the pills down. I watch wordlessly from my pit and have more self-pitying thoughts of dependency, drugs and illness. When the nurse has finished with Moaning Minnie, she comes over to my bed and wheels the blood pressure machine round. I offer my arm but not words. When the rubber sleeve has finished doing its stuff and finally releases the air, the machine bleeps.

"Your heart rate is on the low side," she says.

"Yeah, I'm practically dead," I reply.

The whole procedure is repeated with the same results.

"Are you an athlete?" she asks.

"No, just an Olympic champion in failure," I reply.

The nurse, clearly well-trained and experienced in dealing with narky people like me, just pats my arm, tidies away and tells me that breakfast will come round soon, then quickly apologises when she realises I'm 'Nil by Mouth'. The only breakfast I'll be having is the pre-med.

The rest of the morning goes by in a blur. I've got to the point where I don't really feel, don't really care. Is that what the pre-med has done to me? Or is it because I'm resigned to my own failure of mind and body? Either way, I can't even be bothered to feel sorry for myself, so I just lie and watch without seeing.

When I come round, I'm back in my bed, the curtain drawn around me. There is a blissful moment before I remember, then it all comes flooding back and I realise that there is now an intrusive and unwelcome visitor that lurks underneath the sheets. I don't want to see it, feel it or touch it. If I do that, then it becomes real. A head appears in the gap of the curtains and the young nurse steps through and asks how I'm feeling.

"I'm not," I reply, Miss Narky back in full force.

The nurse explains that she needs to check underneath the covers to make sure everything is ok. She carefully lifts the counterpane, then the sheet and she gasps.

"Is something wrong?" I ask.

"No, it's fine, there was some blood that's all and I thought it was strange, but now I realise what it is."

"I did tell them, they told me not to worry."

The nurse cleans me up and once again I feel like I'm old before my time, losing my dignity and my stance in life, losing everything.

"All done," she says, "everything looks fine. Do you need any painkillers?"

"I don't feel any pain," I reply and I sink into the oblivion of sleep.

My slumber is deep and I dream. The dreams are vivid and disturbing. I'm being chased by a faceless shape, feeling terrified, trying to lock the door but the bolt bouncing back out. I wake up sweating, my heart racing. I try to sit up but the pain almost cuts me in two. There is a faceless shape at the foot of my bed, then the face comes into focus and it's a soulless face. I slump back and close my eyes, not knowing what I want to see less, my nightmares or him.

"How are you feeling?" he asks.

"I'm not," I reply.

He looks puzzled and I want to tell him not to bother trying to figure me out after all these years, it's futile.

"The traffic wasn't too bad, getting here, I was surprised."

"Just go, away" I say, and I close my eyes so that I might drift back to nightmares.

He doesn't move immediately, then I hear the chair scrape and his footsteps echo until all sounds disappear.

CHAPTER 14

The Meeting
2013

Despite the challenges, the transition from respected lawyer to ill person has been surprisingly smooth. It's as if my brain has been reset so that it filters out all the needless detritus and allows only the important stuff through. No longer fretting about missing the morning alarm, deadlines or whether I've got clothes ironed, I now breathe in life and see what's around me. This rubber appendage, which was the cause of much pre-op angst, which farts and stinks like a new-born with colic, has been accepted. It's my 'badge of honour', a reminder that life is transient. If it wasn't for my little 'stink bag', the past would have remained in the darkest caverns of my mind and I might never have experienced the elation of reunion. So, I no longer view this attachment as an intruder, but as an ally. I no longer waste time wishing it wasn't there, but refer to it regularly and with humour. One dark Autumn evening, on leaving my sister's house, she warned me to be careful on my walk to the station. I told her not to worry, one flash of 'dirt bag' and they would run a mile.

These long months of recovery have given me time to reflect on my life and to rethink what went before. Bit by bit, I have allowed past scenarios to unfold so that I can re-examine their meaning in the context of what I now know. I had blocked their content for so long that their meaning became a blurred, distorted and unwelcome image. I think about the time I dropped my phone, when it fell apart, like I was falling apart, when it's power house was separated from its other components so that it no longer functioned. When I reassembled it, all systems were restored and that's how it feels now, for me. I have rebooted my central memory store and reset its default systems. They now allow the downloading of images so that I might look at them again and see them with fresh eyes. I have mulled over the reasons behind my actions and I have tried to understand my younger self, to be a little kinder to her.

A close bond has been formed with the sister who raised me as if I were her own, cemented by our present and past connections. Her perspective on our younger life has helped with my recovery, helped me to see another side to it. Where I shut it out, she kept it alive. Neither way was the right way or the wrong way, just our way. We have laughed and cried our way through memories, taken each one out of its box and held it up to the light. Each painful chapter has been brought before us and we have been judge and jury of it all. For me, it is as if someone has slowly released each screw from the vice around my head, then let the light be absorbed by my body and mind. We have joked about dropping our surnames and changing them by Deed Poll to Freud, as in the psychologist. We share that ability to use humour to salve, even the most painful open sores. Those abusive episodes will never be normalised, never be forgotten, but we are some way to understanding why they happened and why they happened to us.

My future is not something I can easily imagine, not something I can see unfold, it's more uncertain than ever. Having to face my mortality earlier than expected has made me realise how much precious time I have frittered away on things that don't matter. The thought of going into the next world, or into dark oblivion, without reconciling with my child, has become unbearable. I need to see my girl. 'My girl,' the words roll around my tongue and dance in my head, but I'm not brave enough to say them out loud. How can I deserve to call her 'my' anything when, for most of her life, I have been absent? Abandonment of a child by a mother is a pain I would not wish on anyone, and yet I did. I can't absolve myself of that one sin. 'Forgive them Father, for they know not what they do,' well I did know. My childhood years were one long episode of pain and yet I inflicted the same fate on my guileless child. I can only hope that my girl has had the strength and capacity for survival, so that she could come through without too much ill effect. I wish I'd have had someone to shake me up and tell me how stupid I was being to think my child would be better off without me, wish I'd have given someone the chance. I have carried the burden of my actions and inactions for all my life, and it's only in death that I feel strong enough to redress the balance.

I had to leave her to save her and to save myself. For every day of my life, my existence, since that day I ran away, this is what I have told myself. During what I call my 'dark times', my whole being had been swamped by something exterior, something that wasn't physically tangible, but something that made its presence known. Like an ominous dark spectre, it hovered over me, making everything I thought, everything I did into a negative. There were some, including my dear mam, who said I needed to 'snap out of it', if only it were that easy. Comments like that made it easy to blame myself for the moods, for my inability to 'sort myself out'. Nobody knew how they swamped my body, stole my essence, like a magpie after gold. I was too tired, too weak to resist. Feelings of inadequacy soon quashed any merit I dared afford myself for the small achievements. Like a floppy, shiftless puppet, my strings were tweaked and pulled by those around me. They were stronger than me, were so very sure of themselves, confident about their views, about the way they lived their lives. They played on my low self-esteem and they planted seeds which grew into all-invasive entities, into paranoia. If I doubted myself before that episode, then it was reasonable enough to assume that I would doubt myself more when it ended and I did. When the fog had lifted, I could see with more clarity, but by then it was too late. Now, I look back and wish I could return to that time, to those people, hold my baby proudly and with entitlement, show them how different things could have been. If this meeting ever happens, if I'm fortunate to be allowed to atone, I will tell her, 'I had to leave you to save you.'

My sister has been the vital link between my daughter and myself, acting as messenger and counsellor, but most of all the voice of persuasion. She has done a wonderful PR job and I've told her she should have been in politics. It cannot have been an easy task, but, because of her, a meeting has been agreed. All the important milestones and achievements, previously held dear, have been usurped by this one meeting. I'm consumed with excitement and fear, but mostly I'm grateful. If I had to choose one positive outcome from being terminally ill, and there have been a few, it would be that it has given me the courage to get on this train and face my daughter, after all, what have I got to lose?

The train rocks, as if to comfort and calm me, but my stomach churns and I have to sit on my hands to stop them shaking. The voice on the Tannoy announces that the next destination will be Manchester, a place I've avoided, a place with so many connotations of fear. Just hearing the name said out loud throws the churning into overdrive and a tear comes from nowhere. I ease out my hands so that I can rummage in my bag for a tissue. The woman opposite is staring at me and I realise that I must look a mess.

"Are you alright love?"

You wouldn't call me love is you knew what I was.

"Yeah, I'm fine thanks."

"It's just that you've gone pale and you look a bit shaky."

"Do I? I've got an interview and I'm a bit nervous."

Well, it is an interview of sorts.

"Oh, I see. Well, no job's worth getting yourself worked up for. I always think if you do your best and they don't like you, sod 'em."

Good old Northern grit, how I have missed it.

"You're right, thanks, but I really want to get this one."

"Well my advice, for what it's worth is just be yourself."

'And who might that be?' I think, but I smile and she carries on with her reading.

For some reason, when I get off the train and tread once-familiar streets, I think of my own mother, of how she travelled the same paths in her youth and her adulthood. Visions of her with my father come unbidden, of them fighting, her face a mass of bruises and pain and I need to shake them away because they disturb me. I stop to take a breather, thinking what an injustice it is for me to void her like that. I bring back that image and I tell her that I'm so, so sorry.

We've chosen a quiet place to meet, the museum on Whitworth Street. She assures me it won't be busy on a Monday afternoon, neither of us wanted onlookers. I pause on the steps and take the photograph from my pocket. I rub over the pretty face and study those beautiful eyes, try to read what they say. From what I recall, from that lifetime ago, she looks like her dad, the same strong features. I take one last look and tuck it away, then climb the stairs to the entrance. Straight ahead there's an imposing staircase which goes off to the left and to the right. It reminds me of the 'Sliding Doors' scenario again and I can't help but think, 'this is how this meeting will go, one way or the other.' I try to compose myself, tell myself to be positive, then I have a mild panic when I can't remember all the things I'm going to say. I look at my watch, another twenty minutes before the agreed time. Good, I've got time to calm down. I look through the haze for the café sign and see it to the right, so I go through and join the others at the counter. Suddenly cursed by the shakes, I need to steady myself on the bar that holds the trays. 'Where are the trays?' I look around fitfully but someone has joined the line behind me, so I can't come out of my place to get a bloody tray. 'Stop,' I tell myself, 'you're getting worked up again. The lady will help you.' The lady will help me.

"Yes love, what can I get you?"

A Valium? Double G &T? Absolution from my sins?

"A tray please," I blurt.

"Anything else?" she asks, amused.

"A cappuccino please."

"Would you like to try the Rocky Road for an extra pound?"

I splutter, then smile to myself.

"No thanks, I don't think I could stomach it today."

I'm glad that I can still see the funny side of things, it's helped to make me feel a little more human, less trapped. I pay for the drink and find the most remote table for four I can see, tucked away in the corner, thinking a table for two would be too intimate, too constrictive. I set my drink down, the cup rattling in its saucer, spilling the brown liquid over the sides and making a messy puddle. It looks dirty and ugly and I'm trying not to relate it to how I feel, but my thoughts are spiralling down that route, so I look away. Then I see her. An involuntary gasp escapes me, but the irony that she has chosen a table for two doesn't. Without thought, my legs carry me over to her, all shakiness gone and I stand in front of her like the statue of an idiot, mouth aghast and dribbling no doubt, eyes fixed, lips aquiver, feet rooted firmly to the spot. She stands slowly, turns her beautiful face and her graceful body and says

"Mum."

That's all, and I reach to the side of me for a place to sit for a moment before I fall. She scrapes a chair right up next to me and holds both of my hands and I can do nothing but bawl. I bawl quietly, but I bawl ferociously, internalising the sound, my body shaking, once again not my own and she holds both my hands and her beautiful eyes are wrinkled with concern and that's when I take deep breaths so that I can stop, so that I can stop retching and crying and spluttering, so that I can speak to her.

"My girl."

This time I can say it out loud and believe it. This time it's her turn to collapse into herself and sob and shake. I hold her. I hold her very tight and for a long time and people stare, pretending not to, but I don't care, because there is nothing more precious than this moment. We cling and we shudder and we sob and we struggle for breath, then, exhausted, we are stilled and we part slightly and we look. We look at each other, look into eyes that are the same and we see. We see each other's pain and we know. We know that we should have done this a long time ago.

When the tears subside, there is no awkward silence.

"I've missed you so much," I say.

For once I realise the truth. For all these years, for all this time I have tried to forget, to put thoughts of her out of my mind, but my efforts have been futile. Every decision I have made, everything I have done has been an attempt to bury all traces of her so that I could believe she didn't exist at all. Now I understand that if you bury something alive, it will try with all its might to reach the surface.

"I kept seeing you in my head, in your little red shoes with your chubby little legs walking towards me."

She looks at me through tears. "I only had pictures of you. No one really talked about you. They said it was best I didn't know. So, for all that time I have imagined that you were a monster who had done a terrible thing, but really, you're just normal, just my mum."

"For all that time, I had thought myself a monster who had done a terrible thing. It was a terrible thing to leave you Laura, but I thought you were better off without me. I was very poorly, mentally ill. I couldn't see any way out except to leave you so that you could have a peaceful life without me. I'm so sorry. That doesn't seem to be enough, does it?"

"It will take time for me to compute everything, to understand, but I will try. I'm just glad that we've found each other. You were always the missing piece of my life, even though I had a good life. There was always something missing."

"Yes, I know that feeling."

Words don't seem enough and for a moment we just look at each other. Then we fall into easy conversation, just like two old friends. She tells me that she spent a lot of time with her Grandma when she was little, when her dad was working. They would go out on nature walks, so she could name every bird she saw by the time she was five. She speaks with fondness about the woman I thought was my enemy. They would share milk shakes and fries, visit museums or sit for hours colouring in and playing snap. She would tell her stories, take her to nursery, then school, wipe her nose and pull her socks up. At home time, Grandma would greet her with a smile and a treat, 'don't tell your dad.' She tells me that her dad met a lady called Margaret and that they got married when Laura was six. Laura was their bridesmaid and she wore a sparkly dress and silver shoes. I think about that Christmas tree fairy that I once was. She tells me how she knew that Margaret wasn't her 'real' mum, but she chose to call her mum because it made life easier for everyone. For that I am grateful, that my child has had someone who was able to give her what I couldn't, a stable family life.

I tell her about my life in Brighton, how I reinvented myself. I tell her about the job in the bar, how the encouragement of people I met gave me the confidence to go to university. I tell her about the constant battle with myself, with my past, how I had to keep pushing it back in its box. I tell her how I became a lawyer, how I kept myself busy, became respected and sought after, all the while feeling like I didn't belong. I tell her all about the meeting with my sister and my subsequent diagnosis and I tell her that it doesn't look good.

Her face drops and I wonder if I should have been so honest, so quickly.

"Then we'll just have to make the most of the time we have left, mum," she says.

In that one statement, she has summed up everything. We'll just have to make the most of the time we have left, because nothing else matters. We have found each other, rescued each other from the demons in our heads and from now on, life, whatever life we have, will be good.

CHAPTER 15

Marriage, Redemption and Hope
2015

The church is adorned with cream flowers and gold gossamer bows, very classically understated and beautiful. I take my place on the front pew with the closest members of the family and, instead of feeling unworthy, I know that I belong. This is, in no small measure, due to my daughter's unquestioning acceptance of my reappearance. This is the best-case scenario and I am swimming in the joy of it. I am the Mother of the Bride, in my Mother of the Bride outfit, which hangs easily on my skin.

Today, my daughter will give herself completely to another. Today she will commit herself to a new life. Years ago, I would have feared for her safety, for her sanity, but that was then. I have watched them together, seen how much he adores her, how much he wants her to be happy. My joy comes from knowing that she will have a better life than me, that she will break the cycle, that she will be able to love those around her and to accept their love in return, something I could never do. She has the confidence of knowing she is loved and it will carry her through the twists and turns of relationships and life.

I know that, if she ever decides to make a family of her own, she will be a better mother than I could ever be, because she knows how to love. If I think it, I know it will be so. Finally, I can feel some atonement for the biggest sin of my past, for leaving my child. Although misguided and most would say selfish, walking out on her meant that she has had a stable upbringing in a loving home, something I could never have given to her, had I stayed. My in-laws have contributed to that foundation and, now that I see them as they really are, not from my bubble of insecurity, I'm grateful to them. They only wanted what was best for their son, their grandchild and, yes, probably for me. Now my return, albeit tardy, has helped this girl, my daughter, to find the missing piece and fit it back into her life, to gain closure from the past.

The familiar notes of The Wedding March ring out from the organ and intrude my thoughts. Automatically, I turn my head towards the back of the church. Through my tears I can see a vision slowly gliding down this traditional aisle of cream flowers and gossamer bows. It looks as if she is floating, rising above all that has gone before, all that was ugly and untraditional. She is a true Venus. Her father, who has forgiven so easily, looks like any other father walking their daughter down the aisle, proud, joyful, but with a trace of regret for the handing over of this precious life to another. He has told me that it has been easy to forgive, because he has had the honour of bringing up this child of ours and seeing her bloom into adulthood. He even thanked me for allowing him to do that. We both know that it could have been so different had I stayed. It's taken a long time for me to accept that my actions were justified, that they could be forgiven.

It was a different era, one where mental illness was not always acknowledged or understood, one where I was perceived as 'difficult.'

As she passes, she glances at me, a look that holds a thousand words. I know from that look, that my presence is welcome and that her day is complete.

She says she had dreamt about meeting me, had imagined how I might look, had wondered if she looks like me. She says that, although she respected my wish for no contact, she ached for me every day. She says that, even though she doesn't understand what I did, she understands why I did it. I have told her that even I don't understand what I did or why I did it. I have told her that, since the day I left, she has been the last thing I have seen every night, without exception. I told her that I knew about that ache, that I would have given anything to hold her so that the ache would stop. She says that it's made her resilient, that she's had to grow up fast, that she's used the people around her as a substitute for me. Just like I used my job as a substitute for her. She says she's never been happier than she is now. I know that feeling.

I've never been particularly religious, but, as I hear my daughter take her vows, I feel like a celestial body looking down on a perfect life scene and giving it my blessing.

"You may kiss the bride."

I witness the first post-marital kiss and I see that it's full of love, promise, tenderness and joy. It takes all my resolve to stop myself from dissolving into a blithering wreck. The old shame I had felt about breaking those vows threatens to return, but I swallow it down and revel instead in the moment. When the ceremony is over and they walk past me as man and wife, I hope with all my heart that the cycle is broken, that they are strong enough to love and be loved.

Later in the day, at the reception, I notice my son-in-law at the bar. His cheeks are flushed with happiness and alcohol and he is laughing easily with his friends. They seem to be exchanging stories and anecdotes from the past. Sometimes their voices become hushed and I wonder why. Could it be that they're reliving their youth and exchanging tales of past conquests? I suspect so. For some reason, when I see Laura walking towards him, a familiar pang of dread comes from nowhere. I remember my own wedding, a life-time ago. I recall that feeling of being inferior, of not belonging, but that was then and this is now. She nudges in next to him, making a space for herself in his circle of friends, having the confidence that I didn't. She slips her hand around his back and for a moment I hold my breath, almost scared of his response. He returns the affection with a kiss and my fears disappear.

Someone taps me gently on my arm and I turn to see my ex-mother-in-law. I see her in a new light. I see the kindness.

"It's been a while," she says.

"Too long," I say, "much too long."

She places her hand on my arm and squeezes it gently. "It's good to see you, so glad you could be here."

"Thank you. Thank you so much. I want to say thank you, also, for looking after Laura, she idolises you."

"It was my pleasure Alison, she's always been a joy."

"Not like her mother." The comment slips out and I laugh nervously to disguise the heaviness.

"You were confused, like a little girl. We can see that now. I don't think any of us realised how desperate you were, how poorly you were. That will always haunt us. We should have helped you."

"I should have helped myself, Mary. I should have taken the help instead of running away. That will always haunt me."

"We've all been affected in one way or another, but look at her. You only have to look at her to see how happy she is."

She's right. "Thank you," I say, "for your part in her happiness."

"Thank you for coming back. I'm so sorry that it couldn't have been sooner, or in better circumstances, but thank you for coming back."

I never dreamt that this woman, this woman who once looked down on me from the comfort of her class, would ever find it in herself to thank me.

CHAPTER 16

Reflection
2016

Following the wedding, my relationship with my daughter and the rest of my 'forgotten' family continues to develop and we form a close bond. I'm not sure it would have been like this, that I would have had the same response, the same forgiveness and acceptance, if I hadn't been afflicted by this illness, but it doesn't matter. Those months I spent under a cloud of depression, before our meeting, now seem like a waste. She says it wouldn't have made any difference, that she's always wanted to us to meet, but she never had the strength. We can chat easily now and relax without having to explain ourselves. There is nothing to prove on either side, just an acknowledgement that the time we have is limited and we must use it wisely.

When I'm alone, my thoughts take hold and I dwell, for too long, on the past and how it could have been if things had been different, if we weren't enslaved by what went before. Sometimes I wonder what I would say if I could visit myself as a child. How would I help that little mouse, trapped in the circumstance of birth? I see that little girl cowering in a corner or under that scratchy blanket and I cry for the pain and the futility of wasted lives. I think about the marriage I went into with such naivety and so ill-equipped. So young and yet so old. I had missed things I should have had and witnessed things I shouldn't, but it doesn't make my premature departure from those vows any easier to bear. When someone celebrates a big wedding anniversary, I can't help but think 'that should have been me,' can't help but regret that it wasn't. If I had stayed at home, would I have eventually recovered sufficiently to escape my mental imprisonment? I can only speculate. I believed I was saving my daughter from something worse than being brought up by one parent, being brought up by two who couldn't be together, who created ill-feeling and tension, who destroyed each other.

I think about the nature of the illness that stole my young life. It's not that different to the one I have now. It robbed me of the person I was, robbed a child of her mother, a husband of his wife. I was hasty in my retreat, but it was the only thing I saw fit to do. I was deteriorating and I knew I had to get out before I destroyed us all. If I would allow it, my thoughts on the inequity of life would suffocate me, so I need to make sure that I keep my thoughts in check. I don't want a blight of sadness to pervade my present.

For a long time, I have pushed thoughts of her away. It was only the vision of her beautiful little face that remained, that haunted me before sleep took over. Now I have her back. I still feel that I don't deserve her, but we cherish every moment. There have been difficult conversations. It was never going to be easy to step back into a world I chose to leave.

"Did I play any part at all in driving you away mum?"

"That's very difficult for me to answer honestly Laura. All I can tell you is this; that everybody loved you, that you lit up the faces of everyone around you, that you were a pleasure and joy to everyone who knew you."

"If I was so good, wouldn't that have made it easier to be a mum?"

"In normal circumstances yes, but in mine, the fact that everyone else saw you as a joy only served to highlight my sense of failure."

"I'm sorry mum, I don't really understand. I've seen friends under pressure, seen them suffer with depression after having a baby, but if I was good, how could being a mum have affected you so badly?"

"It's complicated Laura. My troubles started long before I became a mum. The pressures of being responsible for another life just served to break me. It sounds so awful to say that motherhood broke me, but it wasn't you, it was the pressure I was under, unseen pressure, the demons in my head. I don't expect you to understand, you have been loved by those around you."

"It's difficult for me to understand how your parents could have hated you, could have ruined your life."

"I'm not sure they hated me, they couldn't love me, that's all. They were so consumed with themselves, they didn't see how they were ruining young lives. They didn't want to see. It's very sad for me to think that I couldn't change history, that I couldn't have set my family on a different route."

"I like to think that you have mum. One thing I do

204

understand is that your leaving gave me a chance to lead a normal life. Maybe I will change history mum, break the cycle."

"Laura, I think you already have."

Chapter 17

Peace
2017

Song on a loop. A silly, inappropriate but then again possibly appropriate song. 'This could be the last time, this could be the last time, may-be the last time, I don't kno -ow, der der de dum.' Who sang that? Can't remember. Was it The Beatles, The Stones, Manfred Mann? Can't think who it was, but it's going around in my head like a ball-bearing in a groove. It's going around in my head because it's almost visiting time. No doubt she's been summoned by 'those in the know.'

I look over at the window to distract myself from the song and the thoughts associated with it. Just the act of looking to the side seems to sap the last of my energy, so I turn my head back again. My arms hang in listless apathy and my legs stick to the bed like they're set in treacle, while muffled voices buzz in my ears. There are other sounds. The slow drip of the morphine and the wheeze of my chest as it rises and falls, reminding me that I'm still here, still 'fighting'. What a stupid word to use. How can you fight something that invades every cell no matter what you do? Drip, drip, bloody drip. You can try to numb the pain but it's always there, always slips through the fog of drugs. It's like the grim reaper himself has come and is tapping at your insides with his scythe.

A blackness closes in from my periphery and I allow it to engulf me, to swallow me whole.

My grandmother sits in front of me, her huge being spilling over the stool as she always did. Her face is softer than I remember. She looks almost sorrowful. I have questions for her.

"What was your story Nanny? Was it the same as mine? Did you ever love my mam? When she was born, did you hold her and have that bond that a mother feels, that overwhelming feeling to protect? When she was two, did you warm to her quirky little ways, or did she always annoy you? Did you and grandad love each other before the madness came? Would you have left him if you could? Would you have walked out on your family like I did? Were you always so cold, so controlling? Did you ever say nice words to her? Did you ever cuddle her, cradle her in your arms and look down at her with tenderness? Did you ever love her, nanny?"

She sits solid in her stool. Her face is soft but she doesn't talk to me. She doesn't talk to me because I can see right into her soul and I can read what's there.

I see pain from a former life. A little girl sits alone on the stone step of a grimy terraced house. Her feet are filthy and her legs are bare. A thin cotton dress and threadbare cardigan are not enough to keep out the chill of a northern winter morning. Her hair is matted and her face wears the grime of the week and a solemn look. She holds the crusted end of a piece of bread as if it is treasure. Her little mouth barely fits around the end of the cob and she struggles to take a bite, gripping the bread in her teeth, then pulling at it so that she can tear a bit off, she chews as if she's never been fed. The door behind her opens and she turns her head and cowers closer to the stone step. A man, her father, swipes her across her pitiful little head and knocks her from the step. He snatches the bread and slams the door. She struggles to her feet. There are no tears, just a haunted look of resignation.

The same little girl lies under a filthy thin sheet in a bug-ridden bed, dreading the night-time visit. The door creaks open and she screws her eyes shut, feigning sleep. When it's over she curls up in a ball and sobs, the words of 'ring-o-roses' going around in a loop in her head. 'Atishoo, atishoo, we all fall down.' It's not the plague that fells us, but our own kin set to destroy us with their own hands.

I see the same girl, a young woman now, searching for safety and finding it in the kind eyes of a young man. I see them walking down the cobbled street. She is slouching and he is telling her to stand tall, but she wraps her cardigan a little tighter and continues to stare down at the ground. He laughs when her body stiffens like an ironing board as he goes to kiss her for the first time. 'I don't bite,' he says and she laughs too. Her fear of intimacy threatens to come between them, but he is patient and he cares about her deeply, so they make plans and they take the vows. Her father 'gives her away,' handing over more than a daughter. When the ceremony is over, there isn't much of a reception as money is tight, so they gather in the village hall for drinks, sandwiches and cake. Her new husband spots her standing in the corner, looking down at the borrowed satin slippers. He tries to slip his arm into the crook of hers, but she hugs it closer to her ribs. He is hurt and he asks what is wrong, but she just shrugs and says she doesn't know, but I can see the fear in her eyes of what might come.

I see the same fear as she looks down at the lump under her apron and he reassures her with an arm around her back and words of encouragement. When the child arrives, she feels a surge of love and an urge to protect. She takes to motherhood easily, washing and cleaning, feeding and rocking the baby, but as the child grows, I see a young mother lost and desolate, overwhelmed by the responsibility of her new role. She questions her abilities as a mother and as a wife, but it's her bed and she must lie in it. She tends to her baby, but her feelings towards the child are ambivalent. I see her slowly deteriorate, beset with the curse of self-doubt, her confidence slowly eroded. I see her shut down bit-by-bit, until she's a mere shell. I see her struggling through the quagmire of each day, existing, not living. The madness takes over and she takes to her bed. People are shunned or welcomed in equal measure. Nobody knows when to approach or when to stay away. She laughs raucously or curses vehemently at the life she's been given. She's a delight and a curse all rolled into one and nobody knows who she is. 'She's a funny one, that.'

She floats away, her imposing body fading and I tell her that I'm sorry. I tell her that I'm sorry for all the things I didn't understand about her and her life. I tell her that I understand now, how her madness took over, how she cut herself off from the child that she bore, that she loved. I tell her that I understand and I tell her for the first time, that I love her.

My mother appears in the faded apron she used to wear when she was baking, the one she used to wipe her hands on when she had to tend to something else, so that it would be covered in smears of margarine and flour. She stands there defiant with that look on her face. Half sneer, half smile.

"Why are you smiling mam?"

She shifts from one foot to the other. Her mouth drops and her face crumples. She is the saddest woman I have ever seen.

"What's up mam?"

But I can see what's up, I can see it in her face and her eyes and the sagging droop of her pitiful body.

I see a child searching for scraps of food and affection in a world devoid of both. She wears a tatty old cotton dress and a knitted cardigan, so shrunken by washing, it resembles felt and is much too tight, even for her scrawny frame. Her mother's face, contorted with hatred, looms over her. She cowers while her mother pokes her in her bony shoulder, reminding her of all the ways in which she is a useless little nothing, each reason punctuated by another poke. She daren't move. Finally, her mother runs out of steam and the child crawls up to bed, sore and bewildered.

I see a young woman crouched like an animal on the floor of her living room. Her cheek burns from the impact of his fist. She tries to get up, but he kicks her down, then he staggers on top of her, his weight pinning her to the ground and crushing her. She tries to move and he rolls off. He bangs his head on the hearth and a trickle of blood oozes from the side of his eye. She doesn't know what to do, so she leaves him there, hoping that by morning he'll be cold. Later, he staggers upstairs and his heavy body slumps beside her. He falls into a deep, drunken sleep. He reeks of stale beer and fags.

Etched in the lines of my mother's face, I see a lifetime of regret and remorse. From that first meeting, she regrets falling for the man who broke her. She is sorry that I was conceived in the worst possible way, born of rape, not love. She is sorry that I was neglected, ignored and ground down by indifference. She's sorry that we had to witness the beatings and the hatred, that she couldn't protect us. She is sorry that she wasn't equipped to stand up for herself until it was too late.

She regrets the selfish decision to leave us with the man who called himself our father but who was neither up to the role, nor wanted it. She's sorry that her new husband didn't like children, didn't make us welcome when we came on the bus to visit. Sorry that she told us not to touch his things, not to make any noise, to be quiet or else it would upset him. She's sorry she never came to meet us at the school gates, just to show that she thought about us. She's sorry that she told us she was too busy when we asked 'why?' She's sorry for her anger at all our questions and she's sorry she wasn't there when there was no food in the cupboard, when my dad rolled in drunk and abusive, my first kiss, my first period, my first heartbreak, my first rape. She's sorry for all of that, I can see it in her eyes.

"Why did you have a favourite mam, was it because he was the first-born? Was there love there at that time, with that first child? Was that before you were beaten and controlled?"

Her mouth forms the word 'No.' It's a very clear no and I'm confused. Then I see it. I see it in her face and her eyes and the pitiful sag of her body. He was special, not because she loved him, but because he was born at a time when she felt loved. She felt love from the man who broke her in the end, because he couldn't love either, but she thought she felt love. It's all clear now. I see a woman who has had to reinvent herself just to survive. I see me.

I don't ask her if she ever loved me or cuddled me or if she felt that surge of love that I felt when my child was born. I don't ask her that. I don't ask her that because I know. I know that she didn't and I know that's where we differ, but I understand. I understand that we pass the wrongs of our upbringing down to our children.

As she floats away, the strings of that bloody apron trailing behind, I tell her for the first time that I love her, and I mean it.

I see a vision of me as a little girl in hand-me-downs searching for cereal, dancing about in bare feet on the cold floor. There's no cereal left this morning and no bread in the house either, my brothers got there first. Once again, I go to school without any breakfast, walk through the iron gate and run across the yard, knowing the whistle would blow at any minute. I trip and my shoe slips off and rolls along the ground. It lands next to a boy and my heart sinks as he picks it up and turns it over. He lets out a howl of laughter and holds the shoe up, calling at all the others to come and look. They too howl with laughter at the bit of cardboard he's removed from inside. He holds the shoe up so that the light shines through the hole in the bottom. The teacher comes over, takes the shoe, takes my hand and leads me away. She finds a spare pair of pumps for me to wear so that I don't have to suffer the humiliation of people pointing at me for the rest of the day, but that's really the least of my worries.

I see myself asleep, curled into the foetal position underneath one thin sheet and a blanket. The door creaks open, but I don't move. I hear the lock being pushed over and the footsteps coming towards the bed. I'm stiff as a board with fear. He gets in next to me and the song on a loop begins in my head. When it's over, he slips away but the song on a loop remains. I don't cry, my tears dried up a long time ago, when I found out no one would listen. I was just a kid who had to get on with it until I could get out.

Everything is clear to me now. My life was destined to motor along a given track, guided by the past. I feel at peace. I feel like all my ducks are in a row. Everyone knows about the whys and the wherefores. Everyone knows why our lives have not been simple. Those who are loved by me know that they are loved. I feel no remorse, no blame, no regret. A sense of calm envelops me and I feel content. Then, I am bathed in gentle light which carries me upwards from where I can see my beautiful girl. She has my hand and she's crying, but she has seen my smile and she knows that I am at peace.

"I love you my darling little one."

Song On A Loop